CRITICS CHEER JULIE GARWOOD'S
FOR THE ROSES

"Ms. Garwood combines the Old West and England to create an incredibly entrancing tale with a cast of unique characters that will certainly linger in your heart. Her gifted prose is always a treat, and *FOR THE ROSES* is no exception."

—*Rendezvous*

"An enchanting tale with a happy ending . . ."

—*Abilene Reporter-News*

"A powerful story about four urchin boys who rescue a baby in New York City, it's filled with characters you'll never forget."

—*Romantic Reader News*

"Lively and charming . . . Filled with humor and appealing characters . . ."

—*Library Journal*

"[A] page-turner filled with lots of family values . . . the reader is never out of Garwood's skillful comfort zone."

—*Kirkus Reviews*

"As wild as the Old West . . . "

—*Publishers Weekly*

"There will be moments when you'll laugh and cry, and others when the warmth and love captured here will enfold you in its powerful embrace. With a master's pen, Julie Garwood explores the heart and soul of a family whose love and loyalty will truly inspire. *FOR THE ROSES* is a brilliant achievement."

—*Romantic Times*

Books by Julie Garwood

Published by POCKET BOOKS

JULIE GARWOOD

One White Rose

POCKET BOOKS

New York   London   Toronto   Sydney   Tokyo   Singapore

This book is a work of fiction. Names, characters, places and incidents are products of the author's imagination or are used fictitiously. Any resemblance to actual events or locales or persons, living or dead, is entirely coincidental.

An *Original* Publication of POCKET BOOKS

POCKET BOOKS, a division of Simon & Schuster Inc.
1230 Avenue of the Americas, New York, NY 10020

Copyright © 1997 by Julie Garwood

ISBN: 0-671-01009-3

First Pocket Books printing July 1997

10 9 8 7 6 5 4 3 2 1

POCKET and colophon are registered trademarks of Simon & Schuster Inc.

Printed in the U.S.A.

One White Rose

Prologue

‏❧

$\mathcal{L}$ong ago there lived a remarkable family. They were the Clayborne brothers, and they were held together by bonds far stronger than blood.

They met when they were boys living on the streets in New York City. Runaway slave Adam, pickpocket Douglas, gunslinger Cole, and con man Travis survived by protecting one another from the older gangs roaming the city. When they found an abandoned baby girl in their alley, they vowed to make a better life for her and headed west.

They eventually settled on a piece of land they named Rosehill, deep in the heart of Montana Territory.

The only guidance they received as they were growing up came from the letters of Adam's mother, Rose. Rose learned about the children from their heartfelt letters to her, for they confided their fears, their hopes and their dreams, and in return she gave them what they had never had before, a mother's unconditional love and acceptance.

In time, each came to know her as his own Mama Rose.

After twenty long years, Rose joined them. Her sons and daughter were finally content. Her arrival was indeed a cause for both celebration and consternation. Her daughter was married to a fine man and expecting her first child, and her sons had grown to be honorable, strong men, each successful in his own right. But Mama Rose wasn't quite satisfied just yet. They had become too settled in their bachelor ways to suit her. Since she believed God helps those who help themselves, there was only one thing left for her to do.

She was going to meddle.

Time of Roses

It was not in the Winter
Our loving lot was cast;
It was the time of roses—
We pluck'd them as we pass'd!

That churlish season never frown'd
On early lovers yet:
O no—the world was newly crown'd
With flowers when first we met!

Thomas Hood (1798–1845)

One

❧

The little woman was in trouble. Big trouble. No one, male or female, pointed a rifle at Douglas Clayborne without paying the consequences, and just as soon as he could get the weapon away from her, he would tell her so.

First, he was going to have to sweet-talk her into stepping out of the stall and into the light. He planned to keep on talking until he had edged close enough to take her by surprise. He'd rip the rifle out of her hands, unload it, and break the damned thing over his knee. Unless it was a Winchester. Then he'd keep it.

He could barely see her now. She was crouched down low behind the gate, shrouded in shadows, with the barrel of the gun resting on the top slat. A kerosene lamp was hooked to a post on the opposite side of the barn, but the light wasn't sufficient for him to see much of anything at all from where he stood, shifting from foot to foot, a few feet inside the open door.

A hard, driving rain was pelting his back. He was soaked through, and so was Brutus, his sorrel. He needed to get the saddle off the animal and dry him down as soon as possible, but what he wanted to do and what the woman would let him do were two different matters.

A bolt of lightning lit up the entrance, followed by a reverberating boom of thunder. Brutus reared up, let out a loud snort, and tossed his head. The horse obviously wanted out of the rain as much as he did.

Douglas kept his attention on the rifle while he tried to soothe the animal with a whispered promise that everything was going to be all right.

"Are you Isabel Grant?"

She answered with a low, guttural groan. He thought his harsh tone had frightened her and was about to try again in a calmer voice when he heard her panting. At first he thought he was mistaken, but the noise got louder. She was panting all right, and that didn't make a lick of sense. The woman hadn't moved a muscle since he'd come inside the barn, so she couldn't possibly be out of breath.

He waited for the panting to subside before he spoke again. "Are you Parker Grant's wife?"

"You know who I am. Go away or I'll shoot you. Leave the door open behind you. I want to watch you ride away."

"Lady, my business is with your husband. If you'll kindly tell me where he is, I'll go talk to him. Didn't he tell you I was coming here? My name is . . ."

She interrupted him in a shout. "I don't care what your name is. You're one of Boyle's men, and that's all I need to know. Get out."

The panic in her voice frustrated the hell out of him. "There isn't any need to get upset. I'm leaving. Will you tell your husband Douglas Clayborne is waiting in town to give him the rest of the money for the Arabian? I'm going to have to see the animal first, as he agreed. Can you remember all that?"

"He sold you a horse?"

"Yes, he did. He sold me an Arabian stallion a couple of months ago."

"You're lying to me," she cried out. "Parker would never have sold either one of my Arabians."

He wasn't in the mood to argue with her. "I've got the papers to prove it. Just tell him, all right?"

"You purchased a horse you've never seen?"

"My brother saw him," he explained. "And his judgment is as good as mine."

She burst into tears. He took a step toward her before he realized he was actually thinking about comforting the woman, and abruptly stopped.

"I'm real sorry your husband didn't tell you about the horse."

"Oh, God, please, not now."

She started panting again. What in blazes was the matter with her? He knew something was wrong, and he had a feeling her husband was responsible for her tears. The man should have told his wife about the horse. Still, her reaction was a bit extreme.

Douglas thought he should say something to help her get past her misery.

"I'm sure all married couples go through spots of trouble now and then. Your husband must have had a good reason for selling the stallion, and he was probably so busy he forgot to tell you about it. That's all."

The panting got louder before it stopped. Then she whimpered low in her throat. The sound reminded him of a wounded animal. He wanted to walk away but knew he couldn't leave her if she was in trouble . . . and just where was good old Parker anyway?

"This shouldn't be happening," she cried out.

"What shouldn't be happening?" he asked.

"Go away," she shouted.

He was stubborn enough to stay right where he was. "I'm not leaving until you tell me who Boyle is. Did he hurt you? You sound like you're in a lot of pain."

Isabel instinctively responded to the concern she heard in his voice. "You aren't working for Boyle?"

"No."

"Prove it to me."

"I can't prove it to you without showing you the letter from your husband and the paper he signed."

"Stay where you are."

Since he hadn't moved an inch, he couldn't understand her need to shout at him. "If you want me to help you, you'll have to tell me what's wrong."

"Everything's wrong."

"You're going to have to be a little more specific."

"He's coming, and it's much too early. Don't you understand? I must have done something wrong. Oh, God, please don't let him come yet."

"Who is coming?" he demanded. He nervously glanced behind him and squinted out into the night. He thought she might be talking about Boyle, whoever in tarnation he was.

He was wrong about that.

"The baby," she cried. "I can feel another contraction."

Douglas felt as though he'd just been punched hard in the stomach. "You're having a baby? *Now?*"

"Yes."

"Ah, lady, don't do that." He didn't realize how foolish his demand was until she told him so between whimpers. His head snapped back. "Are you having a pain now?"

"Yes." She said the word with a long moan.

"For the love of God, take your finger off the trigger and put the rifle down."

She couldn't understand what he was telling her.

The contraction was cresting with such agonizing intensity she could barely stand up. She squeezed her eyes shut and clenched her teeth together while she waited for the pain to stop.

She realized her mistake as soon as she opened her eyes again, but it was already too late. The stranger had vanished. He hadn't left the barn though. His horse was still standing by the door.

The rifle was suddenly snatched out of her hands. With a cry of terror, she backed further into the stall and waited for him to attack.

Everything began to happen in slow motion. The gate squeaked open, but, to her, the sound was a piercing, unending scream. The stranger, a tall, muscular man who seemed to swallow up all the space inside the stall, came toward her. His hair and eyes were dark, his expression was angry . . . and, oh, God, she didn't want him to kill her yet. The baby would die inside her.

Her mind simply couldn't take any more. She took a deep breath to scream, knowing that once she started, she would never be able to stop. *Please, God, understand. I can't do this any longer. I can't . . . I can't. . . .*

He pulled her back from the edge of insanity without saying a word. He simply handed the rifle to her.

"Now, you listen to me," he ordered. "I want you to stop having this baby right now." After giving the harsh and thoroughly unreasonable command, he turned around and walked away.

"Are you leaving?"

"No, I'm not leaving. I'm moving the light so I can see what I'm doing. If you're this close to having a baby, what are you doing in a barn? Shouldn't you be in bed?"

She started panting again. The sound sent chills down his spine.

"I asked you to stop that. The baby can't come now, so just forget about it."

She waited for the contraction to end before she told him he was an idiot.

He secretly agreed. "I just don't want you to do this until I find your husband."

"I'm not doing it on purpose."

"Where's Parker?"

"He's gone."

He let out an expletive. "I had a feeling you were going to tell me that. He picked a fine time to go gallivanting."

"Why are you so angry with me? I'm not going to shoot you."

He wasn't angry; he was scared. He had helped a countless number of animals with their deliveries, but he hadn't helped any women with childbirth and he didn't want to help Isabel Grant now. Oh, yes, he was scared all right, but he was smart enough not to let her know it.

"I'm not angry," he said. "You just took me by surprise. I'll help you back to the house, and then I'll go get the doctor." He hoped to God she wouldn't tell him the town didn't have a physician.

"He can't come here."

Douglas finally got the lamp hooked to the post connected to the stall. He turned around and saw Isabel clearly for the first time. She was an attractive woman, even with the frown on her face. She had freckles across the bridge of her nose, and he had always been partial to women with freckles. He'd always liked red hair too, and hers was a dark, vibrant red that glistened like fire in the light.

She was a married woman he reminded himself, and he shouldn't be noticing her appearance. Still, facts were facts. Isabel Grant was one fine-looking woman.

She was also as big as a house. Noticing that helped

him regain his wits. "Why can't the doctor come here?"

"Sam Boyle won't let him. Dr. Simpson came here once when I was too far along to go into town to see him, but Boyle told him he'd kill him if he ever tried to come to me again. He'd do it too," she added in a whisper. "He's a terrible man. He owns the town and everyone in it. The people are decent, but they do whatever Boyle tells them to do because they're afraid of him. I can't blame them. I'm afraid of him too."

"What's Boyle got against you and your husband?"

"His ranch is next to ours, and he wants to expand so his cattle will have more grazing land. He offered Parker money for the deed, but it was only a pittance compared to what my husband paid for it. He wouldn't have sold it for any amount of money though. This is our home and our dream."

"Isabel, where is Parker now?" As soon as he saw the tears in her eyes, he had his answer. "He's dead, isn't he?"

"Yes. He's buried up on the hill behind the barn. Someone shot him in the back."

"Boyle?"

"Of course."

Douglas leaned back against the post, folded his arms across his chest, and waited for her to compose herself.

She sagged against the wall and lowered her head. She was suddenly so weary she could barely stand up.

He waited another minute before he started questioning her again. "Did the sheriff investigate?"

"Sweet Creek doesn't have a sheriff any longer. Boyle must have run him off before Parker and I moved here."

"No one wants the job, I suppose."

"Would you?" She wiped a tear from her cheek and looked up at him. "Dr. Simpson told me Sweet Creek

1 1

used to be a quiet little town. He and his wife are my friends," she added. "They're both trying to help."

"How?"

"They've sent wires and written letters to all the surrounding towns asking for assistance. The last time I saw the doctor, he told me he had been hearing stories about a U.S. marshal in the area. He believed the lawman was the answer to our prayers. The doctor hadn't been able to locate him yet, but he was certain he would come if he knew how many laws Boyle had broken. I try not to lose hope," she added. "Boyle has at least twenty men working for him, and I think it would take an army of marshals to defeat him."

"I'm sure there's a way to . . ." He stopped in the middle of his sentence, for it had just occurred to him that she had gone several minutes without panting.

"Did the pain go away?"

She looked surprised. She put her hand on her swollen middle and smiled. "Yes, it did. It's gone now."

Thank God, he thought to himself. "You're really all alone here? Don't look at me like that, Isabel. You've got to know by now I don't work for Boyle."

She slowly nodded. "I've learned to be very distrustful. I've been alone for a long time."

He tried not to let her see how appalled he was. A woman in her last months of pregnancy should have been with people who cared about her.

Anger began to simmer inside him. "Has anyone from town looked in on you?"

"Mr. Clayborne, I . . ."

"Douglas," he corrected.

"Douglas, I don't think you understand the severity of my situation. Boyle has the route cut off. No one gets in here without his approval."

He grinned. "I did."

The realization that he had indeed gotten through

made her smile again. Odd, but she was also beginning to feel more in control too.

"Boyle's men must have gone home as soon as it started raining. I think they go back to his ranch every night when the light fades, but I can't be sure."

She straightened away from the wall to brush the dust off her skirt, and suddenly felt her legs give out. She was horrified. She leaned back again so she wouldn't fall to her knees and turned her face away from him as she explained in a whisper what had just happened.

She sounded frightened and ashamed. Douglas immediately went to her side and put his hand on her shoulder in an awkward attempt to comfort her. "It's all right. It's supposed to break." He tried to sound like an authority on the subject. In reality, he had just summed up everything he knew about childbirth with that one simple statement.

"Something's wrong. The baby's not due for at least three to four more weeks. Oh, God, it's all my fault. I shouldn't have scrubbed the floors and done the wash yesterday, but everything was so dirty and I wanted to keep busy so I wouldn't think about having the baby alone. I never should have . . ."

"I'm sure you didn't do anything wrong," he interrupted. "So stop blaming yourself. Some babies decide to come early. That's all."

"Do you think . . ."

"You didn't cause this to happen," he insisted. "The baby's got a mind of his own, and even if you'd been in bed, your water still would have broken. I'm sure of it."

He seemed to know what he was talking about, and she stopped feeling guilty. "I think my baby's going to come tonight."

"Yes," he agreed.

"It's odd. I'm not in any pain."

They were both whispering now. He was trying to be considerate of her feelings. She was trying to get over her embarrassment. The man was a complete stranger, and, oh, God, she wished he were old and ugly. He wasn't though. He was young and extremely handsome. She knew she would probably die of mortification if she let him help her bring her baby into the world, because she would have to take her clothes off and he would see . . .

"Isabel, you about finished hiding from me? You've got to be practical about this. Come on," he coaxed. "Look at me."

It took her a full minute to summon up enough courage to do as he asked. Her face was burning with shame.

"You're going to be practical," he repeated as he lifted her up into his arms.

"What are you doing?"

"Carrying you back to the house. Put your arms around me."

They were eye to eye now. He stared at her freckles. She stared at the ceiling.

"This is awkward," she whispered.

"I don't think the baby cares if his mother feels awkward or not."

He carried her out of the stall, paused long enough to take the rifle away from her and prop it against the post, and then continued on toward the door.

"Be careful," Isabel told him. "The rifle's loaded. It could have gone off when . . ."

"I unloaded it."

She was so surprised she looked him in the eye. "When?"

"Before I gave it back to you. You aren't going to start fretting again, are you?"

"No, but you're going to have to put me down for a minute. I have to take care of Pegasus first."

"Are you talking about the stallion?"

"Yes."

"You're in no condition to get near him."

"You don't understand. He cut his left hind leg, and I need to clean it before it becomes infected. It won't take long."

"I'll take care of him."

"Do you know what to do?"

"Oh, yes. I'm very good with horses."

He felt her relax in his arms. "Douglas?"

"Yes?"

"You're good with women too. I was wondering . . ."

"Yes?"

"About the delivery. Have you ever helped a woman give birth?"

He decided to ease her worry by hedging his answer. "I've had a little experience." *With horses,* he silently added.

"Will you know what to do if something goes wrong?"

"Nothing's going to go wrong." The authority in his voice didn't leave any room for doubts. "I know you're scared and feeling alone . . ."

"I'm not alone . . . Oh, God, you're not going to leave me, are you?"

"Don't get excited. I'm not going anywhere."

She let out a little sigh and tucked her head under his chin as soon as he stepped outside the barn. The rain was still coming down hard, and he was sorry he didn't have anything to wrap around her. The log cabin she called home was approximately fifty yards away, and by the time he had carried her to the door, she was as drenched as he was.

A single lantern provided the only light inside the cabin. The atmosphere was warm and inviting, but what he noticed most of all was the scent of roses that filled the air. To the right of the entrance was an oblong table covered with a yellow-and-white-checked gingham tablecloth, and in its center sat a crystal vase filled with at least a dozen white roses in full bloom. It was obvious she had tried to bring beauty and joy into the stark reality of her life, and the simple, feminine gesture made him ache for her.

The cabin was spotless. A stone fireplace faced the door, and on the mantel was a cluster of silver frames with photographs. A rocking chair with a yellow-and-white-checked cushion had been placed to the left of the hearth and a tall-backed wooden chair with spindly legs sat on the opposite side. Two knitting needles protruded from a burgundy ball of yarn on the footrest, and long strands coiled down to the colorful braided rag rug.

"You've got a real nice place," he said.

"Thank you. I wish my kitchen were larger. I put up the drape to separate it from the main room. It's always such a clutter. I was going to clean it up after I finished in the barn."

"Don't worry about it."

"Did you notice the roses? Aren't they beautiful? They grow wild near the tree line behind the field. Parker planted more on the side of the house, but they haven't taken root yet."

Douglas's practical nature reasserted itself. "You shouldn't have gone out by yourself. You could have fallen."

"It gave me pleasure to bring them inside, and I'm certain the exercise was good for me. I hate being cooped up all day. Please let me stand. I'm feeling fine now."

He did as she requested but continued to hold on to her arm until he was sure she was steady. "What can I do to help?"

"Would you start a fire? I put the wood in the

hearth, but I didn't want to light it until I got back from the barn."

"You carried wood inside?"

"It is my fault the baby's coming early, isn't it? I carried wood down from the hills early this morning. I went back up again this afternoon to collect more. It gets so cold and damp at night . . . I wasn't thinking, and now my baby's going to—"

He interrupted before she could get all worked up again. "Calm down, Isabel. Lots of women do chores right up to the delivery. I was just concerned about the possibility of falling. That's all."

"Then why did you say . . ."

"Falling," he said again. "That's all I was thinking about. You didn't fall, so no harm was done. Now, stop worrying."

She nodded and started across the room. He grabbed hold of her arm, told her to lean on him, and slowed the pace to a crawl.

"It's going to take me an hour to get to the bedroom if you keep treating me like an invalid."

He moved ahead and opened the door. It was pitch black inside.

"Don't move until I get the lantern. I don't want you to—"

"Fall? You seem terribly worried about that possibility."

"No offense, but you're so big in the middle you can't possibly see your own feet. Of course I'm worried you'll fall."

She actually laughed, and she hadn't done that in such a long time.

"You need to get out of your wet clothes," he reminded her.

"There's a pair of candles on the dresser to your right."

He was happy to have something to do. He felt

awkward and totally out of his element. He didn't realize his hands were shaking until he tried to light the candles. It took him three attempts before he succeeded. When he turned around, she was already folding back a colorful quilt on the bed.

"You're drenched. You really need to get out of your wet clothes before you do anything else," he said.

"What about you? Do you have a change of clothes?" she asked.

"In my saddlebags. If you don't need help, I'll start the fire; then I'll go back to the barn and take care of the horses. Have yours been fed?"

"Yes," she answered. "Be careful with Pegasus. He doesn't like strangers." She stared down at the floor with her hands folded together. As Douglas turned to leave, she called out to him, "You're coming back, aren't you?"

She was fretting again. The last thing she needed to worry about now was being left alone. He had a feeling they were in for one hell of a night, and he wanted her to conserve her strength for the more important task ahead.

"You're going to have to trust me."

"Yes . . . I'll try."

She still looked scared. He leaned against the doorframe and tried to think of something to say that would convince her he wasn't going to abandon her.

"It's getting late," she said.

He straightened away from the door and went to her. "Will you do me a favor?"

"Yes."

He pulled the gold watch out of his pocket, unclipped the chain, and handed it to her. The chain dangled down between her fingers.

"This is the most valuable thing I own. My Mama Rose gave it to me, and I don't want anything to happen to it. Pegasus might get in a lucky kick, or I might drop it while I'm drying down my sorrel. Keep it safe for me."

"Oh, yes, I'll keep it safe."

As soon as he had left the room, she pressed the watch against her heart and closed her eyes. She and her baby were safe again, and for the first time in a long while, Isabel felt calm and in control.

Two

❧

She had turned into a raving maniac. She didn't care. She knew she was losing the last shreds of her control, and somewhere in the back of her mind lurked the realization that she wasn't being reasonable. She didn't care about that either.

She wanted to die. It was a cowardly thought, but she wasn't in the mood to feel at all guilty about it. Death would be a welcome respite from the hellish pain she was enduring, and at this stage, when one excruciating cramp was coming right on top of another and another and another, death was all she was interested in thinking about.

Douglas kept telling her everything was going to be just fine, and she decided she wanted to stay alive long enough to kill him. How dare he be so calm and rational? What did he know about anything? He was a man, for the love of God, and as far as she was concerned, he was totally responsible for her agony.

"I don't want to do this any longer, Douglas. Do you hear me? I don't want to do this any longer."

She hadn't whispered her demand. She'd bellowed it.

"Just a few more minutes, Isabel," he promised, his voice a soothing whisper.

She told him to drop dead.

Honest to God, he would have liked to accommodate her. He hated having to watch her in such misery. He felt helpless, inept, and so damned scared, he could barely think what to do.

On the surface, he was presenting a stoic facade, but he wasn't at all certain how long he could keep up the pretense. Any moment now she was bound to notice how his hands were shaking. Then she would probably become afraid again. He much preferred her anger to her fear, and if it made her feel better to rant at him, he wouldn't try to stop her.

She accidentally knocked the water basin over when she threw the wet cloth he'd pressed against her forehead.

"If you were a gentleman, you'd do what I asked."

"Isabel, I'm not going to knock you out."

"Just a little clip under the chin. I need to rest."

He shook his head.

She started crying. "How long has it been? Tell me how long?"

"Just six hours," he answered.

"*Just* six hours? I hate you, Douglas Clayborne."

"I know you do, Isabel."

"I can't do this any longer."

"The contractions are close together now. Soon you'll be holding your baby in your arms."

"I'm not having a baby," she shouted. "I made up my mind, Douglas."

"All right, Isabel. You don't have to have the baby."

"Thank you."

She stopped crying and closed her eyes. She told him she was sorry for all the vile names she had called him. He calculated he had a few minutes left to mop up the water from the floor and go get more towels before another contraction hit. He was pulling the door closed behind him when she called out.

"Leave it open so you can hear me."

She had to be joking. She was shouting loud enough for most of Montana to hear. His ears were still ringing from her last bellow, but he didn't think it would be a good idea to tell her so.

He agreed instead. About three hours earlier, he'd learned not to contradict a woman in pain. Trying to get Isabel to be reasonable was impossible. Oh, yes, it was much easier to agree with everything she said, no matter how outlandish it was.

Douglas carried the porcelain bowl to the curtained alcove Isabel used as a kitchen, grabbed a stack of fresh towels, and headed back. He made it past the hearth before the reality of the situation finally crashed down on him. He had to deliver a baby. He felt the floor shift under his feet. He dropped the towels and slammed back against the wall. Doubling over, he braced his hands on his knees and closed his eyes while he desperately tried to face the inevitable.

His brother Cole had taught him a trick to use when preparing for a shoot-out. Cole said to think of the worst possible situation, put yourself smack in the middle of it, and then picture yourself winning. Douglas had always thought his brother's mental game was a waste of time, but it was all he had now, and he decided to give it a try.

I can do this. Hell with that. I can't do it. No, no, it won't be bad, and I can handle it. All right, I'm standing in front of Tommy's Tavern in Hammond. Five . . . no, ten bloodthirsty killers are waiting for me to come inside. There isn't any choice. I have to go in. I know that, and I'm ready. I know the bastards have all got their weapons drawn and cocked. I can beat them though. I'll get five of them with the gun in my left hand, and the other five with the gun in my right hand while I'm diving for cover. It's going to be as smooth and easy as a drink of fine whiskey. Yeah, I can take them all right.

He drew a deep breath. And I sure as certain can deliver this baby.

Cole's game wasn't working. Douglas was gulping down air now and letting it out faster and faster.

Isabel could feel the beginning of another contraction. This one felt as if it was going to be a doozy. She squeezed her eyes shut in preparation and was about to scream for Douglas when she heard a peculiar noise. It sounded like someone breathing heavily, as though he'd just run a long distance. Douglas? No, it couldn't be Douglas. Dear God, she was imagining things now. It had finally happened; her mind had snapped.

The contraction eased up while she was distracted. A few seconds later, it gained her full attention with a vengeance. She felt as though her body were being shredded into a thousand pieces, and as the spasm intensified, her whimper turned into a bloodcurdling scream.

Douglas was suddenly by her side. He put his arms around her shoulders and lifted her up against him.

"Hold on to me, sugar. Just hold on tight until it stops."

She was sobbing by the time the contraction ended. And then she was immediately struck with another one.

"It's time, Douglas. The baby's coming."

She was right about that. Ten minutes later, he held her son in his arms. The baby was long of limb, deadly pale, and so terribly thin Douglas didn't think the little one had enough strength to open his eyes . . . or last a full day. His breathing was shallow, and when at last he cried, the sound was pitifully weak.

"Is the baby all right?" she whispered.

"It's a boy, Isabel. I'll let you hold him as soon as I get him cleaned up. He's awfully thin," he warned her. "But I'm sure he's going to be fine, just fine."

Douglas didn't know if he was giving her false hope or not. He honestly didn't know how the baby could possibly survive. He was small enough to fit in Douglas's hands, yet he could open and close his eyes and squirm about. Dear Lord, his fingers and toes were so tiny, Douglas was afraid to touch them for fear they'd crumble. He gently shifted his hold and gingerly pressed his fingertip against the baby's chest. He felt the heart beating. How could anything this little be so perfectly formed? It was amazing that the baby could breathe at all. And yet he did.

My God, Douglas thought, *I could accidentally break one of his bones if I'm not careful.* The sheer beauty of God's creation both awed and humbled him. Now Isabel needed one more miracle to keep her son alive.

"You've got to be a fighter, little man," he whispered, his voice thick with emotion.

Isabel heard him. "He'll have help. The sisters told us that every time a baby is born, God sends a guardian angel to watch over him."

Douglas glanced up at her. "I sure hope he gets here soon."

She smiled, for in her heart she knew Parker's guardian angel was already here.

He was holding her son.

It took a good hour to get Isabel and the baby settled. Douglas had to alter the plan to use the cradle her husband had made because when his knee brushed up against the side, the bottom fell out. It was evident Grant had used rotten wood to build the base. Yet even if the wood had been freshly cut, Douglas would still have thrown the contraption out. Nails as long as a man's hand had been driven inward from the outside of the uneven slats, and long, dangerously sharp points angled down toward the bedding. He shuddered to think of the damage those rusty nails could do to an infant.

He was too tired to do anything about it now. He stripped out of his clothes, put on another pair of buckskin pants, and went back to the bedroom to make a temporary bed for the baby. He used the bottom drawer of her dresser and padded it with towels covered with a pillowcase.

By the time he was finished, Isabel was sleeping soundly. The serenity on her face was captivating, and he couldn't turn away. He watched her sleep; he watched her breathe. She was as beautiful and as perfect as her son. Her hair was spread out on the pillow behind her in a tangled mess. She looked like an angel now . . . and not at all like the Beelzebub he had compared her to during her labor.

Another yawn shook him out of his stupor. He carefully transferred the baby to the drawer and was leaving the bedroom when she called to him.

He hurried to her side, forgetting his state of undress. He hadn't put a shirt on yet or bothered to button his pants, but he was more concerned that she was going to tell him the bleeding had increased.

"Is something wrong? You're not . . ."

"I'm fine. Sit down next to me. I want you to tell me the truth and look me in the eyes so I'll know you aren't just telling me what I want to hear. Will my baby make it?"

"I hope so, but I honestly don't know."

"He's so small. I should have carried him much longer."

"He looks like a fighter. Maybe he just needs to put on a little weight."

She visibly relaxed. "Yes, he'll get stronger. Isn't he beautiful? He has black hair, just like his father's."

"Yeah, he's beautiful." She had already asked this question at least five times. "He's still beautiful."

"Shouldn't you bring the cradle into the bedroom?"

"I couldn't use the cradle. It fell apart."

She didn't seem surprised. "What did you do with my baby?"

"I put him in the dresser."

"The dresser?"

He motioned to the bottom drawer. She only had to lean toward him to see her baby. She fell back against the pillow and laughed. "You're resourceful."

"Practical."

"That too. Thank you, Douglas. You were the answer to my prayers."

"No crying, Isabel," he told her. "You need to sleep."

"Will you stay with me for a few minutes . . . please?"

He shifted his position so that his shoulders could rest against the headboard and his legs could stretch out on top of the covers. "Have you decided on a name for your son?"

"Parker," she said, "for his father."

"That's nice."

She heard him yawn again. He was tired, and she shouldn't keep him up with her rambling, yet she couldn't make herself tell him he could leave. She didn't want the intimacy between them to end. They had shared the miracle of birth, and she was feeling closer to him than she had ever felt toward any other man. Her husband would have understood, she knew, and she pictured him now smiling down from heaven upon his son.

Her thoughts returned to Douglas. She was about to ask him where he was going to sleep when she heard his soft snore. She didn't wake him. She edged closer to his side, put her hand in his, and held on tight.

And then she slept.

Three

❧

$\mathcal{D}$ouglas had walked into the middle of a nightmare. He knew Isabel's situation was bad. If what she'd told him the day before was true—and he was certain that it was—then she was in serious trouble. Not only was she being preyed upon by a group of thugs under the direction of a malevolent bastard named Boyle, but she was also completely cut off from town, which meant she couldn't get help or supplies. Last, but certainly just as troublesome, was the fact that she had just given birth. The infant needed her undivided attention, and both mother and son were too weak and vulnerable to be moved.

Then bad got worse. The rain didn't let up. Since dawn, it had alternated between a soft sprinkle and a thundering deluge. He'd become extremely concerned about the weather as soon as he stepped outside in the gray light of day and saw exactly where the log cabin was situated. Last night it had been too dark to see much of anything when he'd ridden down the slope, guided by only a faint flickering light in the field below. He'd already known the cabin was surrounded on three sides by mountains, but what he hadn't known was that her home was sitting smack in the center of the flood floor. Any overflow from the lakes and creeks in the mountains would have to pass through her cabin in order to get to the river below.

He couldn't believe anyone would build a home in such a dangerous spot. Douglas didn't usually speak ill of the dead, but facts were facts, and it was apparent Parker Grant, Senior, had been an incompetent imbecile. Douglas had given Grant the benefit of the doubt when he'd seen the cradle. Some men weren't any good at making furniture. Nothing wrong with that, he'd reasoned. Building a home on a flood path was an altogether different matter.

Still, Douglas didn't want to jump to conclusions. Someone else might have built the place years ago, and Grant might simply have moved his wife inside as a temporary measure until he could build a proper home up on higher ground.

Douglas hoped his guess was right. With any luck— and God only knew she was due for some—Grant had gotten a roof on the new cabin. If it wasn't too far away, Douglas could take Isabel and her son there in a couple of days.

Time wasn't critical yet. Although there were patches of water all over the field behind the house and barn, and the ground was soggy under his feet, he figured he still had some time before they had to leave. There was also the chance that the rain would stop. The usual hot summer sun would quickly dry up the water then, which would give them some additional time.

He needed something to cheer him up, he decided, and so he went to the barn to take care of the horses. He was eager to get a look at the Arabians again. The stallion was as magnificent as his brother had told him he was.

The horse was big for an Arabian, with a beautiful gray coat. Douglas could feel the power in the stallion and the distrust. Isabel had been right, Pegasus didn't like strangers, but fortunately Douglas had always had a way with horses, and once the stallion was used to his scent and his voice, he let him check his injury.

His mate was smaller, somewhat delicate looking, and definitely full of herself. She tossed her head about like a vain woman, which made Douglas like her all the more.

The pair was meant to stay together. As soon as he moved the female into the stall next to the stallion, they nuzzled each other and let Douglas brush them. No wonder Isabel had wanted to keep them. Her husband never should have sold the stallion without first discussing it with her, no matter how desperate he was for money.

The animals' feed was running low. He gave his sorrel and the Arabians as much as they needed, then calculated he had less than a week's ration left.

The supplies inside the cabin were just as sparse. He had only just finished taking inventory when he heard the baby's whimpering. He decided to change him so that Isabel could stay in bed, but when he reached the bedroom door, it was closed.

He knocked twice before she answered him. In a stammer she asked him to please wait until she finished dressing.

"You may come in now."

She was standing by the chest of drawers dressed in a blue robe buttoned to the top of her neck. Parker was nestled in her arms. Isabel was getting prettier by the minute. Douglas realized he was staring at her, glanced away, and noticed then the dress she'd laid out on top of her bed.

"You really should stay in bed."

She finally looked up. The glow of motherhood was still in her eyes, and there was a faint blush on her cheeks. She wasn't looking at him though. Her gaze was directed on the wall to his left.

"Is something wrong?"

"No, nothing's wrong." She sounded nervous. "I want to get dressed and fix your breakfast."

He shook his head. "For God's sake, you just had a baby. I'll fix your breakfast. You sit down in the rocker while I change the bedding."

His voice told her not to argue. She sat more quickly than she should have, and let out a loud moan. "I think I'd better stand up."

He helped her to her feet. She still wouldn't look at him.

"Why are you acting so shy with me?"

Her blush intensified. He shouldn't have been so blunt, he supposed.

"After . . . you know."

"No, I don't know. That's why I asked."

"It's . . . awkward. I was thinking about how I met you and you had to . . . it was necessary for you to . . . when the baby was coming . . ."

He started to laugh. He simply couldn't help it. She didn't appreciate his amusement.

"I was real busy at the time. All I remember is the baby. I was worried I'd drop him."

"Honest?"

"Yes, honest. If it hurts too much to sit down, lean on the dresser until I get your bed ready. The last thing we need now is for you to fall. You've got to be weak."

"Parker's fretful," she stammered out, trying to change the subject.

Douglas leaned closer to her side and peered down at the sleeping infant. Fretful was the last word he would have used to describe the baby.

"He looks real peaceful to me."

They looked at one another and shared a smile. Douglas was the first to turn away, but not before he noticed how pretty her eyes were. They were more gold than brown, and, damn, those freckles of hers were going to keep on distracting him if he continued to stand so close to her.

She had delicate hands too. He had noticed them during her contractions when she tried to choke him because he wouldn't knock her unconscious.

He made quick work of changing the bedding while she listed all the qualities she was sure her son possessed. She started out telling him Parker had already proven how smart he was, and by the time she finished listing his attributes, she had elevated him to genius.

Douglas couldn't figure out how she'd arrived at her conclusions. The baby wasn't a full day old, and all she could possibly know about him was that he slept and he wet.

She was sagging against the chest when Douglas took Parker away from her.

"I could go in the kitchen with you and help you fix breakfast."

"You don't need to," he said. "Is Parker getting enough to eat?"

"He will . . . soon."

"Please, try to get past your embarrassment. I need to know if he's doing all right."

"Yes, he's doing just fine. The doctor spent a long while telling me what to expect. I should be able to feed him by tonight."

He nodded. "If you start bleeding, you'll tell me, won't you?"

"Douglas . . ."

"I'm thinking about Parker," he explained. "Maybe I should go and get the doctor so he can check you. I could sneak him past Boyle's men during the night."

"That isn't necessary. I promised I'd tell you if anything happens."

After he put the baby back in his bed, he helped Isabel out of her robe. Her hands trembled as she tried to get the buttons undone, protesting all the while that she could undress herself. He took over the task anyway.

"I'm not at all tired. I've slept a long time."

She kept on protesting, even after he'd tucked her between the sheets. At her insistence, he checked on her son once more before he left the room, and by the time he pulled the door closed, Isabel was sound asleep.

She ate breakfast early that evening. He fed her burnt toast and lumpy oatmeal sweetened with sugar. He thought it looked pretty good.

She thought it looked awful. Because he'd gone to such trouble to prepare the meal, she ate as much as she could without gagging and thanked him profusely.

After he'd removed the tray, he sat down on the side of the bed to discuss the situation. "We need to talk."

She dropped the napkin onto her lap. "You're leaving."

"Isabel . . ."

"I understand."

Her face had turned stark white. He shook his head. "No, I'm not leaving. I'm going to have to do something about your lack of supplies."

"You are?"

"Yes."

"I could use more flour and sugar. I'm almost out."

"I'm going into town."

"They won't let you come back."

He put his hand on top of hers. "Listen to me. It isn't good for you to get upset. I don't plan to stroll into the general store in the middle of the day. Give me a little more credit than that."

"Then how . . ."

He grinned. "I'm going in during the night."

She looked shocked by the possibility. "You're going to rob Mr. Cooper?"

"We need supplies, and I want to pick up some clothes. I only packed one extra shirt and pair of pants to come here. I'll leave money on the counter."

"Oh, you can't do that. Mr. Cooper will know someone came into the store and he'll tell Boyle. He tells him everything. It's too risky, Douglas. One of them might guess you're helping me. Wait, I know what you can do. Hide the money under the papers on Cooper's desk behind the counter. He'll eventually find it, and it doesn't matter if he ever figures out how it got there. We'll know we didn't steal, and our consciences will be clear. Yes, that's what you should do."

"Why does Cooper tell Boyle everything?"

"He just does," she replied. "So do some of the others. Only a handful of men stood up to Boyle. Dr. Simpson was one of them. He even lied to him for my sake and told him the baby wouldn't be born until the end of September. He was trying to give me more time to figure out a way to get away from Boyle."

"Good. We'll let Boyle keep on believing the lie for as long as possible. Did the doctor ever come out here?"

"Once."

"Did he tell you where the lookouts were?"

"I remember he told me they were lazy because they stay on the hill just outside town, blocking the road leading here. They take turns going back and forth into Sweet Creek."

"I saw those lookouts on my way here. I was wondering if he mentioned any others posted near you. It was dark when I came down the last hills, and I might have missed them."

"I don't think there are any more. There really isn't any reason for them to watch the cabin. They know I can't go into the wilderness. If I tried to go west, it would take over a week to get to the next town. In my condition, I couldn't risk it. No, the only safe way out is through Sweet Creek."

"If they aren't watching the cabin, that's good news."

"Why?"

"The longer I can go without being spotted, the better, and if they aren't watching the field, I can go back and forth from the barn and exercise the horses. I'll make certain Boyle's men haven't changed their lookout points first."

"When will you leave for the general store?"

"As soon as it's dark. Are you going to be okay by yourself?"

"Yes, but it's dangerous for you to go riding in the dark."

"It won't be any problem," he exaggerated. He tried to pull his hand away from hers, but she held on tight. "Tell me everything you know about the layout of the town."

Her memory for details was impressive. She described each building in detail. She even knew exactly where Cooper had his inventory placed inside his store.

"Now tell me where Dr. Simpson's house is located. I want to find out how many men are watching him."

She did as he asked, and then said, "You won't be able to bring much back with you unless you take the buggy, and it's too dangerous. Boyle's men will hear the squeaky wheels."

"I can fix that. You stop worrying, and don't expect

me back before morning. I'll leave the rifle and extra bullets next to your bed . . . just in case Boyle decides to come by. God, Isabel, I hate to leave you, but I . . ."

She threw her arms around his neck. "Please come back. I know you didn't ask for any of this. I'm so sorry I got you involved, but, Douglas, I really hope you'll come back anyway."

He put his arms around her and held her tight. "Calm down. I'm coming back. I promise."

She couldn't seem to let go. She hated herself for being so dependent on him. She had never depended on her husband, but then she had understood his weaknesses. Douglas was the complete opposite of him. Nothing seemed to faze Douglas.

"Parker needs you until I get stronger."

"I'll be back," he promised once again. "You have to let go of me."

"Can I do anything to help you?"

"Sure. Give me a list of the things you need. I don't want to forget anything."

"There's a list in the drawer in the kitchen. I started it weeks ago." She sounded frantic when she added, "I called it my wish list."

He didn't realize she was crying until she released him and sank back against the headboard.

"Ah, sugar. Don't cry."

"I'm just a little emotional today. That's all."

He had to do something to make her trust him. He checked on little Parker, then picked up his pocket watch, told her what time it was, and put it back on the dresser. When he looked at her again, he saw the fear still in her eyes.

"You know what you need, Isabel?"

"It's all down on my list," she answered.

"I'm not talking about supplies."

"Then, no, I don't know what I need."

"Faith. Try finding a little while I'm gone, or you and I are going to have words when I get back."

The hard edge in his voice didn't upset her. She was actually comforted by it. He would come back, if only to give her a piece of his mind for doubting him. He was arrogant and proud enough to do just that, and, oh, it was so wonderful to have him snapping at her. He acted as though he belonged with her and Parker.

"I didn't mean to insult you."

"Well, you did."

She tried to look contrite. She didn't want him to leave on a sour note. "I'll find some faith. I promise." There was a definite sparkle in her eyes when she added, "You be careful, sugar."

Four

❧

Old habits die hard. Douglas had never forgotten
how to pick a lock or get in and out of a building
without being seen. He'd spent several years living on
the streets of New York City, surviving by his wits and
his criminal skills, before he met his three brothers
and his baby sister, and headed west. Before that, he'd
been in an orphanage. Granted, he'd been only a boy
when he'd perfected his criminal technique. But it
was like making love to a woman. After you learned
how, you never forgot.

His experience as a petty thief came in real handy
now. So did the rain, for it kept the night owls inside
their homes. Boyle's men weren't a problem, just an
inconvenience. Douglas stashed the buggy in a cove
near their lair on the hill overlooking Sweet Creek,
then crept up on the four men and listened to their
conversation in hopes of gaining some useful information about their boss. He didn't learn anything

significant. Other than taking Boyle's name in vain several times because he'd assigned them this miserable duty, the men spent the rest of the time boasting to one another about the number of shots of whiskey they could swallow in a single sitting. They were incredibly boring, and after listening to their whining complaints for almost twenty minutes, Douglas hadn't heard anything significant. He was about to make a wide circle around them and continue on when Boyle's men decided to leave their posts and go back into town for the night. Not only had the weather finally gotten to them, but they were also certain their boss would never find out.

Their laziness made Douglas's task easier. He made six trips on his sorrel back and forth from the general store to the buggy with supplies Isabel would need, then headed across town to Dr. Simpson's cottage.

He didn't knock. He went in the back door because, just as Isabel suspected, Boyle was keeping a close watch on the physician. He had a man stationed out front. Douglas spotted the guard leaning against a hitching post across the street with a rifle in one hand and a bottle of liquor in the other. There wasn't anyone watching the back, however. Douglas figured Boyle had ordered one of his men to do just that, but like the complainers up on the hill, he'd probably sneaked home too.

Douglas had forgotten that Isabel had told him Simpson was married. His wife was tucked in nice and tight beside him, sleeping on her side with her back to her husband. All Douglas saw was a puff of gray hair above the covers.

He didn't use his gun to wake the elderly man. He simply put his hand over the doctor's mouth, whispered that he was a friend of Isabel Grant's, and asked him to come downstairs to talk.

The doctor was apparently used to being awakened in the dead of night. Babies, Douglas knew, often came during that inconvenient time. Although the physician seemed wary, he didn't argue with him.

His wife didn't wake up. Simpson shut the door behind him and led Douglas to his study. He pulled the drapes closed and then lit a candle.

"Are you really a friend of Isabel's?"

"Yes, I am."

"And your name?"

"Douglas Clayborne."

"You don't intend to hurt Isabel?"

"No."

The doctor still didn't look convinced.

"I want to help her," Douglas insisted.

"Maybe so, maybe not," Simpson replied. "You aren't from around here, are you? How do you know our Isabel?"

"Actually, I only just met her. Her husband sold me an Arabian stallion a couple of months ago, but I was expanding my business back then and couldn't come for the horse until I'd hired some extra hands."

"But you're a friend. Is that right?"

"Yes."

Simpson stared at him a long minute, slowly rubbing his whiskered jaw until he had worked out whatever it was that was bothering him, and finally nodded. "Good," he said. "She needs a friend as big and hard-looking as you, young man. I hope to God you are hard when it comes to protecting her. You know how to use that gun you're wearing?"

"Yes."

"Are you fast and accurate?"

Douglas felt as though he were undergoing an inquisition but didn't take offense because he knew the physician had Isabel's safety uppermost in his mind. "I'm fast enough."

"I saw your shotgun on the table in the hall," Simpson said. "Are you also good with that weapon?"

Douglas didn't see any harm in being completely honest. "I prefer my shotgun."

"Why is that?"

"It leaves a bigger hole, sir, and if I shoot someone, I shoot to kill."

The doctor grinned. "I expect that's the way it ought to be," he remarked.

He sat down behind his desk and motioned for Douglas to take a seat across from him.

He declined with a shake of his head.

"How's our girl doing? I sure wish I could see her. I expect she's getting big and awkward about now."

"She had the baby last night."

"Good Lord Almighty, she had the baby? It came much too soon. What'd she have? A boy or a girl?"

"A boy."

"Did he make it?"

"Yes, but he's thin, terribly thin . . . and little. His cry is real weak too."

Simpson leaned back in his chair and shook his head. "It's a miracle he survived. Besides being weak, is he acting sick?"

"I don't know if he is or not. He sleeps most of the time."

"Is he nursing?"

"He's trying to," he answered.

"Good. That's real good," he said. "His mama's milk will fatten him up. Tell Isabel to try to nurse him every hour or so until he's stronger. He'll only take a little each time, but that's all right. If the baby refuses to eat, or can't keep it down, then we've got a real problem on our hands. I don't know what good I could do for him if he gets into trouble. He's too young for medicine. We've just got to pray he makes it. A chill will kill him, so you've got to keep him warm all the time. That's real important, son."

"I'll keep him warm."

"I don't want to sound grim . . . It's just, you have to understand and accept the facts. There's a good chance the baby won't make it, no matter what you do."

"I don't want to think about that possibility."

"If it happens, you have to help Isabel get through it. That's what friends do."

"Yes, I will."

"How is she doing? Did she have any problems I should know about?"

"She had a difficult time with the laboring. She looks all right now."

"You helped her bring the baby?"

"Yes."

"Did she tear?"

"No, but she sure bled a lot. I don't know if it was more than what's expected. I've never delivered a baby before. I ask her how she's doing, and that seems to embarrass her and she refuses to talk about it."

The doctor nodded. "If she were in real trouble, she'd tell you for her son's sake. Try to keep her calm, and be real careful about upsetting her. Isabel's a strong woman, but she's vulnerable now. New mothers tend to become emotional, and I don't expect Isabel to be any different. The least little thing might set her off, and she doesn't need to be fretting about anything. Paul Morgan's wife cried for a full month. She plumb drove her husband to distraction worrying about her. The woman cried when she was happy and when she was sad. There wasn't any rhyme or reason to it. Eventually she snapped out of it. Isabel's got more serious problems to deal with. I don't know how I'd stand it if I had Boyle breathing down my neck. I'm sure worried about her son though, coming early like he did, and I know she must be worried too. If the baby makes it, are you planning to stay with our girl until he can be moved?"

"Yes, I'm staying. How long do you think that will be?"

"At least eight weeks, but ten would be even better if he's slow to put on weight. I'm mighty curious about something, son. How'd you manage to get to Isabel's ranch in the first place?"

"It was dark and I was taking the most direct route, using the moonlight to guide me, until it disappeared and the rain started. I almost ran into Boyle's lookouts by accident then. They were so drunk they didn't hear me. I wondered what they were doing hiding out in the rain," he admitted with a shrug. "But I wasn't curious enough to find out. I'm glad now I didn't stop."

"It was dangerous riding down the mountain path in the dark."

"I took my time, walked some of the way, and the light in Isabel's window provided a beacon for me."

"Are you sure you can get back to her tonight?"

"I'm sure."

"I wish I were younger and more agile. I'd try to get to Isabel in the dark too, but I don't dare chance it at my age. I was never very good with horses. They scare me," he admitted. "I've fallen more than I care to recollect. Now I use a buggy, and my wife helps me rig the horses up every morning. Besides, even if I could get there, Boyle might hear about it and then my Trudy would get hurt. No, I can't chance it, but I thank the Lord you came along."

"You told me there wasn't anything you could do for the baby now," Douglas reminded him.

"I could be a comfort to Isabel. She's like a daughter to Trudy and me. After Parker died, I asked her to move in with us, but she wouldn't hear of it. She's determined to stand on her own two feet. Trudy pleaded with her to at least stay with us until after the baby was born; then Boyle got wind of our plans and put a stop to it. My wife found a nice little cottage down the road from us, and we wanted Isabel to consider moving in there and raising her baby in Sweet Creek. She'd be as independent as she wanted, yet close enough that we could lend a hand every now and then."

The doctor's affection for Isabel made Douglas like him all the more. "I'll take good care of her and the baby," he promised.

"Have you noticed how pretty she is yet?"

Douglas felt like laughing, so absurd was the question. "Yes, I noticed."

"Then I've got to ask you what your intentions are, son."

The question blindsided him. "Excuse me?"

"I'm going to be blunt, and I expect I'll rile you. Still, I've got to ask. After she recovers from childbirth, do you plan on dallying with her?"

He'd never heard it put quite that way before. "No."

Simpson didn't look convinced. He suggested Douglas pour each of them a shot of brandy, waited until he'd given him a glass, and then leaned back in his chair to think about the situation. "It might happen anyway," he remarked

"I've only known Isabel for—"

Simpson interrupted him. "You just promised me you'd stay with her for ten weeks, remember? You're a man of your word aren't you?"

"Yes, and I will stay, but that doesn't mean I'll . . ."

"Son, let me tell you about a man I happened to run into in River's Bend."

Douglas could feel his frustration mounting. He didn't want to hear a story now. He wanted to talk about Boyle and get as much information about the man as he could.

The doctor wasn't going to be rushed, if the way he sipped his brandy and stared off into space were any indication. Age gave the older man the benefit of Douglas's attention and respect, and so Douglas leaned against the side of the desk and waited for the tale to be told.

It took Simpson over thirty minutes to tell his story about three couples who got stranded in a snowstorm and stayed together in a miner's shack for the entire winter. By the time the spring thaw came, the six of them had formed what the doctor called an undying friendship. Yet five years later, he happened to meet one of the survivors and asked him several questions. To the doctor's amazement, the gentleman couldn't remember the name of one of the men he'd spent the winter with.

"That's the point of my story," Simpson said. "Yes, sir, it is. You're going to be living close to Isabel for a long time, and I want you to remember the fella I just told you about. He pledged his friendship, went so far as to call the other two men his brothers, yet once he got on with his life, he plumb forgot about them."

"I understand," Douglas said.

"Do you? Isabel has a good heart, and she sure is an easy person to love. It's the future I'm worried about, after you take care of this business with Boyle and go back home. You are going to do something about the tyrant, aren't you?"

Simpson had finally gotten to the topic Douglas wanted to discuss. "It seems I am," he said. "Tell me what you know about Boyle."

"I know the man's a monster." His voice echoed his disgust. "The only reason I'm still breathing is that he thinks he might have need of my services in the future. He's threatened to kill me, but I don't think he'd do it. Doctors are hard to come by in these parts. He'd hurt my Trudy though. Yes, he would."

"Isabel told me that only a few men in this town have had the courage to stand up to Boyle and that you were one of them. Why won't the others help?"

"Everyone that I know would like to help, but they're afraid. They've seen what happens to those good men who have tried. If one of them so much as whispers about doing something to help Isabel, word gets back to Boyle, and then the instigator gets hurt bad. Both of Wendell Border's hands were broken after he told a couple of men he thought were his friends that he was going to find the U.S. marshal everyone's been hearing glory tales about. The lawman was scouring the territory, looking for some wanted men, but Wendell never got the chance to go hunting for him. Boyle's men got to poor Wendell before he could even leave town. While I was setting his broken hands, I promised him in a whisper that I'd find a way to get help here. I promised him I'd pray too."

"Were you going to go hunting for the lawman?"

"No, I'm too old and worn out to go hunting for anyone. My Trudy, fortunately, came up with a better idea. Twice a week I go into Liddyville to see patients there. It's only two hours away from Sweet Creek by buggy," he added. "My wife told me to use the telegraph office there and send wires to all the sheriffs in the territory. She thinks one or two might want to help us. I took it a step further and sent wires to two preachers Wendell told me about and asked them to help with the hunt for the marshal. I still haven't heard back from anyone, but I've got this feeling that if the Texan hears about our trouble, he'll come, especially if he knows a mother with a brand-new baby needs help. Why, he'll drop everything and come running."

"Why do you think—"

Simpson wouldn't let him finish his question. "If the rumors are true, the marshal accidentally caused some women and children to get killed during a bank robbery in Texas. He didn't know they were inside and being used as shields when he and his men rushed in. From what we've heard about the robbers, they would have killed them anyway, but the marshal still blames himself. Oh, he'll come all right . . . if he hears of our trouble. Sure wish I knew the fella's name. It would make chasing him down easier, I expect."

"You're looking for Daniel Ryan," Douglas told him. "My brothers have been searching for him too." He paused when he heard the creak of the steps behind him. "Did we wake your wife?"

"No, but she's used to snuggling up against me and she must have awakened when she got cold."

"Would you mind telling her to put the gun down?"

Simpson was astonished. "Do you have eyes in the back of your head? Trudy, put that away and come in here. I want you to meet Isabel's friend. He's promised to help our girl."

Douglas turned around and nodded to the woman. "I'm sorry I disturbed you and your husband," he began.

Trudy laid the gun on the desk and rushed forward to shake Douglas's hand. Her grip was surprisingly strong for a woman her size, for the top of her head barely reached his shoulders.

"The doctor and I were praying for a miracle. Looks like we might have gotten one. I know you aren't Marshal Ryan. You're big like we were told he was, but you don't have yellow hair and blue eyes, and our preacher gave us a good description of the lawman so we'd recognize him if he came into town. We pray every Sunday that the dear man will hear of our troubles and come here. Could you be a friend of the marshal's? Did he send you here?"

"No, ma'am, he didn't send me here."

She couldn't hide her disappointment. "But you're still going to help our little girl?"

Douglas smiled. The Simpsons' affection for Isabel pleased him. God only knew, she needed good friends now, and it was nice to know she had two champions in Sweet Creek trying to look out for her.

"Yes, I'm going to help her."

She squeezed his hand before she let go. "Doctor, I expect I'll go into the kitchen now." She waited until her husband nodded agreement before she looked at Douglas again. "You won't be leaving until I've packed some leftovers for you to take."

"You'll have to work in the dark, Trudy," her husband told her.

"I expect I'll manage. I'll light a candle and put it in the hallway. No one can see inside, doctor."

"Ma'am, I really should be heading back to Isabel."

She shook her head at him and left the library in a near run.

Simpson chuckled. "You might as well relax, son. Trudy isn't going to let you leave without a bag full of her home cooking. Sit on down in a chair, proper like, and tell me why your brothers have been searching for the Texan. Do you have troubles where you come from that need the law?"

"No," Douglas answered. "Ryan helped one of my brothers. The fact is, he saved Travis's life."

"So you're wanting to thank him."

"Yes, but also get back a compass he . . . borrowed."

"Now, that sounds like a mighty curious tale."

"I'll tell you all about it some other time," Douglas promised. "When I was coming here, I noticed your town has a wire service, and I was wondering why you had to go to Liddyville to send your telegrams."

"The only way you could have seen the telegraph office is if you'd been inside the general store. It's in the back room. Why'd you go in there?"

"To get some supplies."

"Did anyone see you?"

"No."

"Good," Simpson whispered. "You broke in, didn't you?"

"Yes."

"Did you snap the lock or break a window?"

Douglas was a bit insulted by the question. "No, of course not. Cooper won't know I was there unless he does a close inventory."

Simpson was grinning with pleasure. "I hope you robbed Vernon Cooper blind. His brother, Jasper, runs the wire office, and both the scoundrels are in Boyle's back pocket. No one in Sweet Creek dares send a wire from here unless they want Boyle to know about it, and that's why I used the wire service in Liddyville. Just on principle Trudy and I get all our supplies there too. We'd rather go without than give either one of the Coopers our hard-earned money."

"If Ryan were to show up and arrest Boyle, would the man whose hands were broken testify against him?"

Simpson shook his head. "I expect Ryan will have to find another way to get rid of Boyle," he said, "or run his henchmen out of town first. Wendell's too scared to testify. He's got a wife and two young daughters. He doesn't dare say a word against Boyle, or his family will pay the consequences. The poor man. He's got crops that will be ready to harvest in a couple of weeks, and with broken hands he's going to have to watch them rot."

"Won't some of the town help him?"

"They're afraid to do anything that might make Boyle mad."

"Why does he want Isabel's land?"

"He's telling everyone he wants to put his cattle there to graze. He has a lot of land surrounding his ranch house, but he rents that out to some foreigners who buy cattle down in Texas and have them brought up to his land to fatten up. Boyle's made a fortune over the last fifteen years, but he's greedy, and he wants more."

"If he wants to use Isabel's land, why doesn't he do it? She couldn't stop him, and he has to know that."

"He doesn't just want her land, son, he wants her too. He's real blatant about letting everyone know she's going to belong to him. Why, he struts around town like a fat rooster inviting people to the wedding. Folks say he started lusting after her the second he saw her."

"Why is he waiting? He could force her to marry him now."

"You don't understand Boyle the way I do. Pride's involved. He wants her to beg him to marry her, and he figures if he makes her desperate enough, she'll do just that."

"Did he kill her husband?"

"If the bullet hadn't gone through his back, I would have suspected Parker accidentally killed himself. I'm not speaking ill of the dead, you understand. I'm only stating facts, and the fact is that Isabel's husband was about as useful as a kettle with a hole in the bottom. The man had grand notions about all sorts of things. He treated Isabel good though, real good. And he was kind to crazy old Paddy, even though he knew Boyle would hear of it and be furious."

Douglas was intrigued. "Being kind to an old man infuriated Boyle?"

"It's perplexing, isn't it? Paddy came to Sweet Creek straight from Ireland and had lived here for as long as I could remember. Boyle came along about ten years ago and squatted on the land adjacent to where Isabel is living now. Within a year he started building himself a grand three-story house, and when it was finished, it was as fancy as any you'll see in the East, I'll wager you. He filled it with new furniture he had shipped from Europe and then had a big party the whole town was invited to so he could show off the palace. Even Paddy was invited, but something happened that night that started the feud between the two men. No one recollects seeing the two of them together during the shindig, but from that night on, Boyle tormented Paddy with a vengeance. Folks started calling the Irishman crazy then because no matter how often Boyle came after him, Paddy laughed about it. You know what that crazy man told me while I was patching him up one evening? He said he was going to have the last laugh. Can you imagine? The funny thing is, he did."

"How'd he do that?"

"Well now, I'm getting to that, son. Paddy was dying of consumption. He hung on until one Saturday night, because he knew that was when Boyle always went to the saloon to play cards. I happened to be there that night too, and I'll tell you it was the strangest dying I've ever seen. Paddy had dragged himself out of his sickbed, came into the saloon, and then laid down on the floor. He folded his hands together on top of his chest as though he was already in his coffin and announced he was going to die in a few minutes. That's when things turned mighty peculiar. Boyle knocked a chair over running to the old man. He knelt down beside him, waving me and everyone else away, and then he grabbed hold of Paddy's shirt and began to shake him, shouting, 'Tell me, old man. Tell me who it is.'"

"What happened then?" Douglas demanded to know, fascinated by the bizarre story.

"It got even more peculiar, son, that's what happened. Paddy gave Boyle a big toothless smile and whispered something only Boyle could hear. And then he laughed. As God is my witness, Paddy died laughing. Boyle went crazy. He started choking the dead man and screaming vile names at him. Two of his men had to pull him off the Irishman so the funeral cart could come and collect him, and I heard one of his men ask him why he hadn't killed Paddy years ago. Boyle was still reeling from whatever it was the Irishman had said to him, and all he would mutter was that he couldn't kill him without knowing. The following day Trudy and I went to say our good-bye to old Paddy, and I swear to you when I looked in that coffin, that crazy old man had a big smile on his face. Isn't that the darnedest story you ever heard?"

Douglas agreed with a nod. The doctor let out a loud sigh, and then said, "Boyle got over whatever was bothering him as quick as could be and started in pestering Isabel and Parker Grant the following week. No one saw him kill Parker, but everyone believes he did. I expect he thought our girl would fall right into his hands then, being pregnant and helpless and all. That was his big mistake because there isn't anything helpless about Isabel. Naturally she's vulnerable because of the baby, and I figure Boyle, with all his money and power, thought he could snatch her right up."

"Does he have marriage in mind?"

"Oh, he wants her legal," Simpson replied. "Since she hasn't started begging him yet, we think he's waiting for the baby to come along. He's a smart one, Boyle is. Most mothers will do anything to feed their little ones. Isabel's a fine woman, but too pretty for her own good. I lied to Boyle, told him the baby wouldn't come until the end of September, and Isabel didn't start showing until she was well into her fifth month, so Boyle has no reason to think I'm lying. I don't know if the extra time will help much, but I'm hoping Boyle will continue to leave her alone until he sees for himself that the baby's here."

"Doctor, the food's packed up," Trudy called from the hallway.

Simpson immediately stood up. "What else can I do to help?" he asked.

"I'd appreciate it if you'd send a wire to my brothers telling them I'll be delayed."

The doctor motioned to some paper and a pen. "You write it all down, and I'll see to it first thing in the morning."

"Do you usually go to Liddyville on Mondays to see patients?"

"No, Tuesdays and Fridays are my usual days, but I could come up with a reason to go early."

"There isn't any need for that. Besides, you shouldn't change your routine."

"Are you planning to bring in some help soon?"

"Yes."

"I expected you would," he replied. "I ought to mention something important first. Boyle's going to be leaving to attend his annual family gathering in the Dakotas. He's never missed one in all the years he's lived here, and everyone expects him to leave real soon. You don't want him to bring more men back with him, and I know he'll do just that if he gets word Isabel has evened out the odds. Besides, it's too risky to move the baby now, and you don't want to be worrying about Boyle's men setting her place on fire. They'll do it as sure as thunder follows lightning if they know you're inside."

"How long will Boyle be away?"

"It varies from year to year. There's just no telling. Last year he was gone six weeks, but the year before he was back in a month. I heard it's a big family get-together he attends, and because he's considered to be the most successful of all the relations, he likes to stay a spell to get their adulation."

"I'm going to write down a second message I want you to send when the time comes, and I want you to promise me that if you hear from Ryan, you'll let me know. I'd like to have a word with him."

"How am I going to get word to you?"

"I'm going to come back every Monday night to check in with you."

"Just to find out if I've heard from the marshal? Son, that sounds like you're getting false hopes up. The chances of locating him are mighty slim."

Douglas shook his head. "That isn't my main reason for checking in with you, sir. If I don't show up, you'll know something's wrong, and that's when I want you to send the second telegram. Do you understand?"

"I do," he agreed. "You'll be careful coming back here?"

"Yes," he promised. "I wish there was a way I could get Isabel and the baby to you and your wife though."

"You'd be bringing trouble to town if you tried. Boyle checks in on her, and I'm sure that one of his men will take over the duty while he's gone. If she isn't where she's supposed to be, they'll tear this town apart looking for her. It won't do any good to take them to Liddyville because he's got friends there too, and there isn't another town close enough to be safe for that newborn. You've just got to stay put, son. If you don't let Boyle's men see you, they'll continue to leave Isabel alone. You don't want that monster coming after you. No, sir, you don't."

Douglas didn't agree. "Just as soon as Isabel and her son are safe, I'm going to want Boyle to come after me. Fact is, I'm looking forward to it."

The doctor felt a cold draft permeate his bones. Isabel's champion had smiled when he made his last comment, but his eyes told another story. They were cold . . . deadly.

Simpson took a step back before he realized he didn't have to be afraid. He followed Douglas into the kitchen and whispered additional advice. "When the time comes, you'll need help, son. There are twenty-four men working the ranch for Boyle, and every one of them is no good riffraff looking for trouble. With Boyle leading them, that makes twenty-five in all."

"I'm not worried. My brothers will come."

Simpson's wife heard the remark. "How many brothers are in your family?" she asked.

"Five now, including my brother-in-law."

Simpson looked incredulous. "Five against twenty-five?"

Douglas grinned. "It's more than enough."

Five

Douglas didn't make it back to the ranch until almost dawn. Before he unloaded the supplies and bedded down the sorrel, he hurried to the cabin to check on Isabel and the baby.

She was standing in front of the fireplace with the rifle up and ready. When he called her name and softly knocked, she ran to the door, unbolted the lock, and threw herself into his arms. She didn't mind at all that he was drenched from head to foot.

"I'm so happy you're home."

Her arms were wrapped tightly around his waist. He felt the barrel of the rifle against his back and quickly reached behind him to take it away from her. She continued to hug him while he leaned to the side and put the weapon on the table.

"I couldn't imagine what was taking you so long," she whispered. "But I never once thought you wouldn't come back."

"I'm glad to hear it," he said. "You're shaking. If you'll let go of me, I'll add another log to the fire. New mothers have to be careful. You don't want to get sick."

She didn't want to let go of him. "I'm not cold . . . I'm just very relieved you're back. Douglas, I was worried about you."

She was trembling almost violently now. He held on to her so she couldn't fall down.

"I was worried about you too," he admitted.

Her face was hidden against his chest. "Did you have any trouble?"

"None at all," he replied. "I got everything on your wish list and a few extras as well. Then I went over to see Dr. Simpson."

"But Boyle told me his men are watching his cottage night and day," she cried out in alarm.

"They never saw me," he assured her. "I met the doctor's wife too. She packed up a bag of food and fresh milk for you."

"Oh, that was nice of her."

"The doctor sent lots of advice."

She was patting his chest. He wondered if she realized what she was doing.

"You're very resourceful, Douglas." *And reliable,* she silently added. "How did you manage to get in and out of the general store and Simpson's house without being seen? Did you break the locks?"

"No, I just jimmied them open."

"Good heavens, how did you learn to do that?"

"I was a thief a long, long time ago."

For some reason, she found his admission hilarious. He didn't know what to make of her reaction. He liked her laugh though. It was filled with such joy.

He forced himself to focus on more practical matters. Pulling away from her, he took hold of her hand and led her back to her bed. "Have you been up long?"

"Most of the night," she admitted. "So was the baby. He just went back to sleep."

"Dr. Simpson wants you to try to feed him every hour or so. Is he nursing yet?"

"Yes," she answered.

"Do you think he got enough milk?"

"Yes," she answered. "He kept it down too."

She sounded proud of her accomplishment, yet also shy about it. He caught her looking up at him, shared a smile, and then told her to go to sleep.

"Couldn't I help you unload the supplies?"

"No."

"Oh, I almost forgot. I fixed your breakfast. It's on the counter."

"I'll eat after I've put everything away and taken care of Brutus."

"Did you remember to leave money for Mr. Cooper? I've never stolen anything in my life, and I'm not about to start now."

"I left exactly what he deserved."

Technically he hadn't lied to her. He hadn't told her the truth either, yet he didn't feel guilty about it. He had left Vernon Cooper what he owed him, which was nothing, not a single penny. Cooper had turned his back on Isabel and joined ranks with Boyle, and as far as Douglas was concerned, Vernon and his brother, Jasper, the disreputable telegraph man, should be run out of town. Only then would they get what they really deserved.

Isabel was too excited to sleep, but she pretended to do just that so Douglas would bring in the supplies. Her excitement increased each time she heard him come back inside. She kept count by how often the floorboard in front of the hearth squeaked. Twelve wonderful times she heard the creaking sound, and that meant six trips to the kitchen and six trips back to the buggy. Were his arms filled, or was he carrying in one bag at a time?

Waiting was blissfully excruciating. Finally, she heard the buggy being driven back to the barn, and she couldn't bear the suspense another second. She threw the covers off, put on her robe and her slippers, and tiptoed into the living room.

She let out a gasp of joy then, for the table and four chairs were stacked high with bags, and there were more on the floor as well. She ran to the table and gasped once again when she saw a large crock of butter, real butter, and another crock filled with coffee. Her fingertips caressed each and every bag, and everywhere she turned, she saw something even more wonderful to cry about. There was beef jerky and ham and bacon and four giant pickles wrapped in white paper. Pickle juice was dripping onto the tablecloth, and she thought that was a most beautiful sight, indeed.

She glanced up and saw Douglas watching her. He was standing in the door, and in his arm was yet another bag. She wondered what he was thinking. He had the strangest look on his face, as though he didn't know what to make of the sight, but there was such tenderness in his eyes, she knew she didn't need to worry that he might be angry with her for getting out of bed.

"I didn't know you were there," she said.

"I was watching you. You remind me of a little girl on Christmas morning." His voice was filled with compassion. How long had she gone without the basic necessities every man and woman were entitled to, he wondered, and did she realize she was hugging a bag of flour? Or that she was crying?

"There's more on the counter."

"More?" she cried out.

It seemed to be too much for her to take in. She stood there frozen with the flour wrapped tight in her arms and stared down at her treasures on the table.

"Come and see," he suggested.

She didn't put the flour down but carried it with her to the alcove. He reached up to push the floor-length drape further to one side on the rope and tried to step back so she could see inside. The kitchen was too narrow for both of them, but she wouldn't give him time to get out of her way. She squeezed herself past him.

Then she gasped yet again. "Salt and pepper and cinnamon and . . . oh, Douglas, could we afford all this?"

She was pressed against him with her face turned up to his. A man could get lost in those beautiful freckles and incredible golden brown eyes.

"Could we?" she asked again in a breathless whisper.

The question jarred him out of his fantasy. "Could we what?"

"Afford all this."

"Yeah," he drawled out. "Cooper was having a sale." He managed to tell the lie without laughing.

"Oh, that was nice."

They kept staring at each other. He reached over and slowly wiped away the tears from her cheeks with his fingers.

She surprised him by leaning up on tiptoes and kissing him.

"What was that for?"

"Being so good to me and my son. I'm sure I'll get my strength back real soon. I've never really depended on anyone before, not ever. It's very nice though. Thank you."

She turned to leave. He followed her, reached over her shoulder, and took the bag of flour away. "What about your husband? Didn't you depend on him every once in a while?"

"Parker had fine qualities. I'm sorry you didn't know him. I'm certain you would have liked him. He really was a good man, Douglas. Good night."

He watched her walk away. She hadn't answered his question, and he wasn't certain if it had been a deliberate evasion or not. He decided he was too tired to ask her again. He went back to the barn to dry down his sorrel, then used a clean bucket of rainwater to give himself a good scrubbing before he finally headed to bed.

He slept most of the day away on his bedroll in front of the hearth. Parker eventually jarred him awake with a bellow guaranteed to make his mama snap to attention. His cry wasn't at all puny, but forceful. Was the infant already getting stronger?

Isabel's laughter rang out. She was in the kitchen giving Parker his first full bath.

Douglas joined her. "He's louder today," he remarked with a yawn.

"He's angry."

Douglas noticed the baby was shivering and remembered Dr. Simpson's advice to keep him as warm as possible. "I should have kept the fire in the hearth going."

"You needed to sleep."

"Are you about finished? I don't want the baby to get cold."

Her full attention was centered on Parker. "There, he's clean again. Hush now," she crooned to the baby. "It's all over. Douglas, will you grab that towel for me?"

He hurried to do as she asked. He spread the towel over his bare shoulder, reached for Parker, and laid him up against it. Isabel used another towel to pat him dry. A minute later she was securing his diaper when Douglas noticed Parker's lips were turning blue.

"We have to get him warm quick. Unbutton your robe and your gown."

She didn't hesitate. "He feels like ice," she whispered in alarm. "I shouldn't have bathed him. He's so cold, he can't even cry now."

"He'll be warm in a minute," he promised. He wrapped the gown and the robe around her, draped a clean diaper over Parker's fuzzy black head, and stood there frowning down at him. "Tell me when he stops shivering."

She was afraid to move. "It's all my fault. What was I thinking?"

"That your son was rank," he told her. "Next time, we'll bathe him together in front of the fire."

"He stopped."

"Shivering?"

"Yes. I think he's asleep." She let out a happy little sigh.

Douglas lifted the diaper away from Parker's head to see his face. "Yeah, he's sleeping," he whispered.

And his face was pressed against freckles. "He's a lucky man."

"Little man," she corrected. She blushed as she looked up at Douglas. "Yes, he is lucky, and so am I to have you here."

"You aren't going to cry, are you?"

"Oh, I never cry."

He thought she was joking, but she didn't laugh.

"It's very difficult for me to show any emotions. Haven't you noticed?"

"Can't say that I have."

"Could you do a favor for me? A couple of the chairs have wobbly legs, and I'd appreciate it if you would show me how to fix them. I'm not sure if I should nail the legs to the base or if I should—"

"I'll fix them," he promised. "Anything else?"

It turned out she had quite a list of repairs she needed. Although it was foolish for him to fix furniture that she wasn't going to be able to take with her when she left, he decided to do the repairs anyway. He wouldn't discuss the future with her yet, purposely waiting until she was stronger and less emotional, for even he could see that childbirth had left her physically and mentally exhausted. Dr. Simpson had told him she shouldn't get upset. Besides, the chores would keep him busy.

"Are Boyle's men watching the cabin?" she asked.

"They weren't last night, but they could have moved closer by now. I'm not going to take the chance. The doctor suggested I stay hidden during the day and work at night, but I had already decided to do just that. As long as Boyle believes you're all alone, he'll hopefully be content to wait."

"What about the horses? They can't stay cooped inside the barn all the time."

"I'll exercise them during the night. I'll start rebuilding the corral as soon as it's dark. Stop worrying."

"What can I do to help?"

"Get stronger."

She would have argued with him if Parker hadn't demanded her attention.

Cooking wasn't one of Douglas's talents, and so he sliced the ham and bread Trudy Simpson had sent, and opened a jar of pickled beets he'd stolen from the general store. He gave Isabel a full glass of milk. She wanted to save it and would have insisted if he hadn't told her he could easily get more.

She returned to the main room an hour later with Parker up against her shoulder and watched Douglas repair a chair while she paced with the fretful baby. Douglas noticed how exhausted she looked and decided to leave the other chairs until tomorrow night. He washed his hands and then took the baby from her.

"I'll walk with him."

"I don't know what's wrong with him. He's been fed and changed and burped, but he still won't go to sleep."

"He's just being ornery."

She started to turn away, then changed her mind. "I'll sit up with you and—"

"You don't need to," he said. "If I get into trouble, I know where to find you."

"You're certain nothing's wrong with him?"

"I'm certain."

"Good night then."

Douglas sat down in the rocker and began to gently pat the baby's back. He remembered how he used to rock his sister, and Lord, how fast time had moved. Soon now Mary Rose would be rocking her own son or daughter. Douglas used to talk things over with his sister while he rocked her, and he did the same thing now with Parker. The vibration of his voice had calmed Mary Rose, or bored her, into sleep. The reason really didn't matter; the result was always the same. Parker settled down within minutes and was snoring like an old man.

It was dark now and time for Douglas to get some work done. He braced himself for the anger he would feel the second he stepped out the door. Sure as certain, he got mad, because he was again reminded that the cabin was sitting in the center of the flood line. He couldn't seem to move past that appalling realization. It didn't matter to him that her dead husband might not have built the cabin, or that he might have moved his pregnant wife into the quarters as a temporary home while he built a cabin on higher ground. The man had still put Isabel in danger. Why in God's name had he done it? Didn't he care?

Grant's incompetence didn't stop there. He'd built a corral—at least that was what Douglas thought it was supposed to be—but apparently the first strong wind had knocked half of it down. He was pretty certain Pegasus had sustained his leg injury by accidentally brushing up against one of its exposed nails. If that was true, the risk of serious infection increased considerably. Douglas had to find out as soon as possible, so that he could change the salve he was applying to Pegasus if he needed to, but he decided to wait until morning and let Isabel get as much sleep as possible.

It was a little after dawn when she joined him at the table. She had Parker snuggled in her arms.

A fire crackled in the hearth and gave the room a nice warm glow. Douglas stood up and pulled a chair out for her.

She noticed the lumpy oatmeal and the burned toast he'd again prepared.

He noticed how her hair was shining in the light coming from the fire. She wore it in a long braid down her back. Curly red strands had escaped the binding and framed the sides of her face, and damn but she was a fine-looking woman. Motherhood agreed with her.

She realized he was staring at her and grew self-conscious in no time at all. "Parker won't burp." It was all she could think of to say to take his mind off her unkempt appearance.

He threw a clean towel up against his shoulder and took the baby from her. "Can you sit at the table?"

"Yes. I'm feeling better now."

Douglas stood over her while he gently patted the baby's back. Isabel didn't want to hurt his feelings by refusing to eat the unappealing food, and so she forced half of it down with big gulps of water. She wanted to save the rest of the milk for supper.

"You should be drinking milk with every meal. I'll bring more back next Monday."

"We did have two milking cows several months ago."

"What happened to them?"

"I'm not sure. They were here one morning, and gone the next."

"Do you think Boyle stole them?"

She shrugged. "Parker didn't seem to be overly upset about it, and he refused to talk about it much. I think he might have forgotten to close the stall doors. He was a bit absentminded."

"Are you telling me they might have wandered away?"

"The barn door might have been left open too," she said, staring down at the table. She seemed embarrassed, and for that reason, he let the topic go. He turned away from her so she wouldn't see his astonishment. Honest to God, her husband hadn't been worth the price of air.

"What about the cabin? Parker didn't build it, did he?"

"No, he didn't. How did you know that?"

It was well-constructed, and that was how he knew her husband couldn't have built it. He didn't answer her question for fear of upsetting her though, and asked another one instead. "Was he building a home for you up on higher ground?"

"No. What an odd question to ask. We moved in here."

She tried to get up from the table then, but he put his hand on her shoulder to make her stay. "Finish your breakfast. You need to regain your strength. Tell me, how did Pegasus get hurt?"

"Some of Boyle's men were shooting their guns in the air, and Pegasus reared up against the barn door."

"Was it an exposed nail that cut him?"

"No, it wasn't."

The baby drew their attention with a belch worthy of an outlaw. Isabel's smile made Douglas think she believed her son had just accomplished an amazing feat.

"I really can't eat another bite," she protested. "I'll save the food for later." She stood up before he could argue with her. "I'd like to prepare supper tonight. I just love to cook," she exaggerated. "It's . . . soothing. Yes, it's soothing."

He wasn't buying her lie. He burst into laughter and shook his head at her. "The oatmeal's that bad?"

Her eyes sparkled with devilment. "It tastes like cement."

They stared into one another's eyes for what seemed an eternity, and neither one of them wanted to look away.

"You've really got to stop doing that."

The huskiness in his voice made her feel warm all over. "Doing what?" she asked in a breathless whisper.

"Getting prettier every day."

"Oh." She sighed the word.

He realized what was happening before she did. He was also staring at her freckles again and quickly forced himself to look out the window instead. A movement near the tree line suddenly caught his attention. He froze. There was a shadow slowly moving down the path toward the field. He was still too far away for Douglas to see his face, but Douglas knew who was coming. The lone rider had to be Boyle. Dr. Simpson had warned him that the predator liked to look in on the woman he was terrorizing. Oh, yes, it was Boyle all right.

Douglas's first concern was that Isabel not panic. She'd wake up the baby then, and Boyle would move his men in. Douglas continued to stare at the shadow and made his voice sound as mild as Parker's snore when he spoke to her. "Isabel, will the baby sleep for a while?"

"Oh, yes. He was up most of the night. He has to catch up on his sleep today."

She took the baby away from him and headed for the bedroom. He followed her, waited until Parker was all tucked in, and then calmly told her company was coming.

Isabel didn't panic. She began to undress instead. "How much time do I have?" she asked. She threw her robe on the bed and started unbuttoning her nightgown.

"What are you doing?"

"I have to get dressed and go outside."

"The hell you do. You're staying in here."

"Douglas, be sensible. If he sees me, he'll go away. I always go out on the stoop with my rifle. I want him to see me pregnant. I'll need a belt. Will you get one of Parker's out of the box in the corner? Don't stand there. We have to hurry. He doesn't like to be kept waiting."

"You are not . . ."

She ran to him and put her finger over his mouth to stop his protest. "If I don't go out, he'll start shooting his gun in the air. The noise is going to wake Parker. Do you want him to hear the baby? Now, help me get dressed so I can placate the man. Please."

He pulled her hand away from his mouth and held on to her. "It's out of the question. I'm going out and kill the bastard. You got that?"

"No."

"It'll be a fair fight," he promised. "I'll make him draw."

She frantically shook her head at him. "Stop being so stubborn. Boyle won't be drawn into a fight. The man's a coward, Douglas. There isn't time to argue about this. You can protect me just fine from the front window. If he looks like he's going to hurt me, then you can come outside and make him leave. You aren't going to kill him though. Do you understand me?" The set of his jaw told her he didn't understand. "Please? Restrain yourself for my sake. All right?"

"Honest to God, I sure would like to—"

She stopped him cold by touching his cheek. "But you won't."

He wouldn't agree or disagree. "Maybe," was all he would allow.

She rolled her eyes heavenward. "The belt, please. Get the belt."

He took his own off and handed it to her. "You're not wearing anything that belonged to Parker."

The issue seemed to matter to him, and since his pants stayed put on the tilt of his hips, she didn't waste time arguing.

As soon as he went back to the window to check Boyle's progress, she got ready. She was still swollen around the middle, but not nearly enough to look as though she were drawing close to the delivery date she and Dr. Simpson had given Boyle.

She joined Douglas as Boyle was just reaching the flat at the base of the hill.

"Do I look as pregnant as I'm supposed to be?"

"I guess so."

She put her hand on his arm. "You're supposed to look at me before you decide."

He finally gave her a quick once-over. He didn't like what he saw and frowned to let her know exactly how he felt. Isabel was dressed in a white blouse and a dark blue jersey jumper that ballooned out around her middle, and in his opinion, she was too attractive for the bastard to see. Was she deliberately trying to entice him? No, of course she wasn't. She couldn't help being pretty, and unfortunately, he couldn't come up with any ideas to radically change her appearance . . . unless she was willing to wear a burlap bag over her head. He didn't bother to suggest it though, because he knew she wouldn't do it.

"Button up your blouse."

"It is buttoned."

"Not the top two," he said. He put his gun back in his holster and took over the chore. "He isn't going to see any more of you than he has to," he told her.

His fingers rubbed against the bottom of her chin. How in heaven's name could any woman have such silky skin?

"He won't hurt me," she whispered.

His gaze moved to hers. "I'll make certain he doesn't hurt you. If I have to kill him, I don't want to hear any argument. Agreed?"

"Yes."

"Come on then. He's coming up to the cabin."

She reached for the doorknob, her attention on Douglas while she waited for him to get into position by the window. She didn't wait for him to give her permission to go outside because she knew she'd stand there the rest of the day if she wanted the stubborn man to give her his approval.

"I'm going out now."

"Isabel?"

"Yes?"

"Don't you dare smile at him."

$\mathcal{S}ix$

❧

$\mathcal{B}$oyle was as ugly as sin. His face was covered with pockmarks, his eyes were set too close together, and his lips all but disappeared when he closed his mouth. The man looked like a chicken. Douglas wasn't surprised by his appearance though. The fact that he had to resort to terrorizing a woman in order to get married indicated the bastard had a serious problem attracting the fairer sex, and most women who had learned to look deeper would have been sickened by the evil lurking inside.

Douglas willed the man to move his hand toward his gun. Boyle wouldn't accommodate him. He didn't even bother to glance toward the window, but kept his gaze firmly directed on his prey.

Isabel held her own against him. "I told you to get off of my land. Now, get . . ."

"Is that any way to talk to your future husband, girl? And me planning a real party wedding for you.

You're looking worried today. Are you getting scared about birthing that thing all alone?"

"You've got ten seconds to leave or I'll use this rifle."

"You'd go to prison if you did."

"No jury would ever convict me. Everyone in Sweet Creek hates you as much as I do. Now, leave me alone."

He pointed his finger at her. "You watch your tongue around me, girl. I don't like sass. You've still got your fire inside you, and I'm going to have to do something about that after we're hitched. You will beg me to marry you, you know. It's only a matter of time."

She was cocking the rifle when he dug the spurs into his horse and rode away.

"I'll be back," he shouted. The threat was followed by his grating laughter.

Douglas kept Boyle in his sights until he was halfway across the field. Isabel came inside, shut the door softly behind her, and sagged against it.

"Damn, he's ugly," he muttered.

She nodded agreement. "He won't come back for another two weeks."

"Maybe," he allowed. "We're still going to be prepared for anything. Dr. Simpson told me Boyle will be leaving for some kind of family get-together."

"He's going away? Oh, Douglas, that's wonderful news."

"Simpson said he usually stays a month to six weeks with his family in the Dakotas. We aren't going to let our guard down or get lackadaisical."

"No, of course not. May I ask you something?"

He kept his gaze on the shadow starting up the path. "Sure."

"Won't you look at me?" she asked.

"Not until Boyle goes over the rise."

"I don't understand what's come over you. You told me you didn't want to let Boyle see you and that as long as he continues to think I'm all alone, he'll be content to wait. . . ."

"That was before I knew you always went outside to speak to him."

"But—"

"I don't like it."

She rolled her eyes heavenward. "Obviously not," she replied. "I'm still going to continue to go out every time he comes here, like it or not."

"We'll discuss it later. You shouldn't get upset, Isabel. The doctor said it isn't good for you."

"For heaven's sake, I'm not sick. Surely you've noticed I'm getting much stronger every hour. So is my son."

"Eight weeks from the minute Parker arrived," he announced with authority. "That's how long it will take him to get stronger."

"Surely not."

"Eight weeks," he stubbornly insisted.

"When will you be leaving?"

He smiled. "In eight weeks, unless you or Parker gets into trouble. Maybe longer. And by the way, Isabel, you and your son are going with me. I'm getting you out of here."

"No, you're not. I won't be run out of my own home. Do you understand me? No one is going to chase me off of my land."

Too late, he realized he'd upset her. Her voice had taken on a shrill quality, and when he looked at her, he saw the tears brimming in her eyes. He quickly tried to calm her.

"You can do what you want," he lied. "As long as it's eight weeks from now."

"You can't possibly stay here that long. I assure you I'll be fully recovered sooner than that and Parker will be much stronger. We'll be just fine. We'll miss you, of course." *Desperately so,* she silently added.

He didn't know what compelled him to do it, but he

leaned down and kissed her forehead. "You seem to be having trouble grasping numbers, sugar. I'm not leaving for eight weeks. Want me to tell you how many days that is?"

She knew he was teasing her but didn't have the faintest idea how to respond. Her husband had always been terribly serious about everything. He never flirted, nor did she, yet she knew Douglas was now doing just that. She decided to get away from him for a few minutes. She couldn't seem to think when he was so close.

"It's your decision," she said. "I won't be plagued by guilt, and if you don't mind staying, I . . . I mean to say, we . . . I *have* a baby, you know, and we'll be happy to have you around." She knew she was stammering her explanation. She'd also lied to him. She wouldn't be happy if he stayed. She would be ecstatic.

"Why don't you take your nap now?"

He was saying something to her, but she couldn't make herself pay any attention. She was trying to figure out how such a ruggedly handsome man had managed to remain unattached so long. He had to be close to thirty if her guess was right. Perhaps he wasn't unattached after all. There could be a beautiful young lady patiently waiting for his return. Yes, that was it. She was probably very refined and elegant too, and Isabel imagined she had gold-colored hair that wasn't at all unruly with curls.

"Why did you kiss me?" she blurted out.

"I felt like it. Did you mind?"

"No . . . I didn't mind."

She told herself to snap out of her stupor. It was high time she faced a few important facts. She wasn't a naive young lady with hopes and dreams and yearnings to be loved. She was a widow with a baby who depended on her. She couldn't and wouldn't change her past. She had been blessed to have a dear friend for a companion, and now she had his beautiful son.

Still, there wasn't any harm in daydreaming about a future she could never have, was there? Wasn't it natural to wonder what it would feel like to be loved by a man like Douglas? Thinking about it seemed like a natural curiosity on her part. That was all. He was so strong and hard and sensual, and she'd never known anyone quite like him. Why, even though she was a new mother and didn't physically want him, she couldn't help but notice the erotic, earthy aura about him. Besides, there wasn't anything wrong with appreciating the wonderful differences between them, and, Lord, he was masculine all right.

He'd be a demanding lover, and he wouldn't stop until she had . . .

Good Lord, what was she doing? She forced the outrageous fantasy out of her mind.

"I believe I'll rest for a little while." He looked as if he was amused by her remark.

"Sounds good to me," he teased.

She turned, stumbled over something littering the floor, and yet hurried on. He followed her.

"Are you feeling all right?" he asked.

"Yes."

"You seem a little preoccupied."

"I need a nap, Douglas. I'm a brand-new mother and I must rest."

He leaned against the doorframe and refused to budge when she tried to shut the door.

"I would like some privacy so that I can change my clothes. I'll give you your belt back later."

"It's on the floor in the other room with the towels you used to look pregnant."

She didn't believe him until she put her hand on her waist. Good Lord, when had they fallen, and why hadn't she noticed?

"Want to tell me what you were thinking about a minute ago?"

She could feel herself blushing. "This and that."

"Is that what you call it?" he asked.

"The horses," she blurted out at the very same time. "Minerva and Pegasus. Yes, the Arabian stallion is Pegasus and his mate is Minerva. Didn't I tell you their names already?"

"Just Pegasus."

She really wished he would go away for a little while. The way he was looking at her was making her feel self-conscious and as awkward as a little girl. "What have you been calling my Arabians?"

"This and that."

He slowly brushed the back of his fingers down her cheek. "I think you should know something. I'm real partial to women with freckles. Yours drive me wild." He leaned down and kissed her on the mouth quick and hard. "By the way," he whispered, "I'm having some real wild thoughts about you too."

He stunned the breath out of her, and he knew it. That was why he winked at her before he turned around and walked away. She stared after him until he disappeared into the kitchen; then she shut the door and fell back against it. Dear God, he'd known all the while what she was thinking about, and she was never, ever going to be able to look at him again.

She was mortified. She must have given herself away, but how in heaven's name had she done that? She didn't know, and she wasn't going to ask him. She wasn't going to have another scandalous thought about him for the rest of her life. In fact, she wouldn't think about him at all.

She threw herself down on the bed and groaned. She fell asleep a few minutes later with her feet hanging over the side of the bed, her shoes and stockings on, and one thought flitting through her mind.

He liked freckles.

Seven

He also liked games. He asked her during supper if she happened to have a deck of cards, which she did, and then he suggested they play poker.

"Have you ever played five card stud?"

"Oh, yes. I'm good too."

The challenge was issued. They played five hands before Parker demanded to be fed. It was past time for her to go to bed anyway, because she was looking as though she was about to doze off any minute.

At her insistence, he added up their scores and told her the amount she owed him.

She stood up, yawned, and said, "I'll pay you back with my earnings tomorrow night when we play chess."

He laughed. "Are you good at chess too?"

"Wait and see."

Chess was his game. The following evening, he proved it to her by destroying her in a matter of minutes. He decided she obviously hadn't played a lot of checkers after he'd won five games in a row. By the end of the week, she owed him over a thousand dollars.

Douglas changed the rules from then on. He told her he had a much better idea. Instead of money, the winner could ask any question he or she wanted. No matter how personal the topic, an answer was required.

Suddenly, her skills improved. She won three games before he caught on to her ploy.

"You were deliberately letting me win, weren't you?"

"Some men like to win."

"Most men like to win fairly. From now on, we both play to win. Agreed?"

"Yes," she replied. "We should probably start all over. I let you win last night too."

He tore up the sheet of paper with the totals before handing the deck of cards to her. She shuffled the cards like a dealer in Tommy's saloon, drawing a laugh from him.

"You little con."

"I've played a lot of cards," she admitted.

"No kidding."

She proved how good she was by winning the next game. Before he had even showed her his pitiful hand consisting of two jacks, she asked her question.

"You told me you were a thief, remember? I want to know when and where."

"When I was a boy, living on the streets of New York City. I took pretty much anything I wanted."

Her eyes widened in disbelief, yet her voice sounded as though she was in awe of his criminal background. "Did you ever get caught?"

"No, I never got caught. I was lucky."

After she'd won the following game, she asked him

to tell her about his family. He explained how he, Travis, Cole, and Adam had joined together to become a family when they found a baby in a trash pile.

Isabel was fascinated, asked him a countless number of questions, and before he realized it, he'd talked for over an hour. By the time he was finished, he'd told her about his sister's husband, Harrison, and Travis's new bride, Emily. He saved the best for last and spoke in a soft voice when he talked about his Mama Rose.

"You know it's kind of odd really, now that I think about it, but Mama Rose is the reason I'm here. She heard about the Arabians and wanted me to come and see them. I was too busy at the time, and so I asked Travis to stop by the auction for me."

"Parker was going to sell Pegasus at an auction? That can't be true. The only time he left Sweet Creek was to go to an attorney's office way up in River's Bend. Paddy went with him, and I'm certain they both came back here right away."

Too late, Douglas realized he'd brought up a sore topic. "They probably stopped to rest their horses, that's all. By the way, Dr. Simpson told me about Paddy. Was he really crazy?"

"No, but everyone in town thought he was. He just had a few peculiarities. I got to know him quite well because he came to supper at least four times a week. He was much closer to Parker though. The two of them would put their heads together and talk in whispers well into the night. It was an odd friendship."

"Did Parker ever tell you what they talked about?"

"No, he was very secretive about it, so I didn't pester him to tell me. He said he'd promised Paddy not to discuss whatever plans they were hatching. I miss the Irishman. He had such a good heart. Did you know he was here before Sweet Creek was even a town?"

"No, I didn't," he said. "Tell me, did Parker keep other secrets from you?"

"If you're thinking he was going to sell Pegasus behind my back, you're wrong. Parker and I grew up together at an orphanage near Chicago, and I know everything there is to know about him. He wouldn't have done such a thing. He knew how much the horses meant to me. The sisters at the orphanage gave them to me so that I would have a dowry when I left them."

"Where did they get the Arabians?"

"They were donated to the orphanage by a man they took in. He was dying, and it was his way of thanking them, I suppose. He didn't have any relatives, and he was terrified of dying alone. The sisters sat with him day and night."

Douglas could see she was getting melancholy and quickly turned the topic. "Have I satisfied your curiosity about my family?"

She stopped frowning and shook her head. "How did Travis meet his wife, Emily?"

Douglas answered her question, and by the time he was finished, she was smiling again. It was obvious she had put the matter of Parker's selling Pegasus out of her mind for the moment.

"Does everyone like Emily?"

There was a yearning quality in her voice he didn't quite understand. Was she worried about the newest member of their family? If so, why?

"Yes, we all like her very much."

"I'm sure I would like her too," she said with a yawn she couldn't contain. "We should probably stop now. Could we play cards tomorrow night?"

"After I repair all the chairs. I still have three more to fix."

"You don't need to worry about that. I already fixed them."

He looked surprised. "Honestly, Douglas, I'm not helpless. I did a good job too. See for yourself."

He didn't believe her until he checked them. "You did a better job than I did."

"I watched you, remember?"

He did remember. He was impressed too that she would take the time and trouble after he had promised to do the task for her.

"Your eyelids are drooping now. You're sleepy, aren't you?"

"Yes. Good night, Douglas."

"Good night, sugar."

The next four weeks didn't drag. Douglas was surprised by how quickly the time passed and how comfortable he became in Isabel's home. He felt as though he were part of a family, and while that was a bit disturbing to him, it was also very, very nice.

He kept busy from sundown to sunup. Once a week he risked being seen during the day to hunt for fresh meat and to fish in a stream he'd found in the mountains west of the ranch. Every night he rode Brutus up into the hills to check on Boyle's lookouts to make certain there hadn't been any changes in their positions or numbers. When he returned to the ranch, he kept up with the ordinary chores, such as cutting wood and cleaning stalls.

His relationship with Isabel underwent a subtle change. In the beginning he'd deliberately teased her to make her feel good and smile. Now he teased her because her smiles made him feel good. He wasn't certain when it had happened, but he wasn't thinking of her as a new mother any longer. She had turned into a wonderfully sexy woman with all the right curves. Everything about her aroused him. He liked the way she spoke, the way she moved, the way she laughed. Dr. Simpson had been right when he'd said that Isabel was an easy woman to love. Douglas recognized that his heart was in jeopardy but couldn't figure out how to stop the inevitable from happening.

Like an old married couple, the two of them played cards every evening until it was dark enough for him to go outside. Several nights Parker joined them, and they took turns holding him while they played. Isabel won more games than he did, until he finally stopped staring at her freckles and started paying attention to what he was doing.

Boyle was way overdue for his next check on Isabel, and Douglas was getting edgy thinking about the bastard. He wanted to put an end to the terror tactics the coward used against her.

"You just won a game. Why are you frowning?"

"I was thinking about Boyle. He's late checking on you. You told me he usually comes here every other week to see you. . . ."

"He usually does," she agreed.

"Then why hasn't he? I know he hasn't left for the Dakotas yet because every Monday night when I check in with Dr. Simpson, that's the first question I ask him. Why is Boyle dragging his feet?"

"I don't know, but I don't want to think about him now. We'll be ready for him if he comes calling. Ask me your question so we can play another hand before Parker wants to be fed again."

"Why did you name the Arabians Pegasus and Minerva?"

"I was fascinated by mythology when I was in school. I used to draw pictures of Pegasus all the time. According to the legends, he was a beautiful white horse with majestic wings. Minerva was the Roman goddess of wisdom, and the sisters at the orphanage were constantly telling me I could certainly use a little wisdom. I didn't have much common sense back then," she thought to add. "Anyway, Minerva caught Pegasus and tamed him. I found that very romantic."

She covered her mouth, sneezed, then apologized.

"You don't need to apologize," he said. "Tell me something. Did Parker catch you the way Minerva caught Pegasus, or did you catch Parker?"

"It wasn't like that with Parker and me. We were best friends for as long as I can remember. The sisters at the orphanage called him their little dreamer. I'm sure they meant it as a compliment, because Parker had such a kind heart. He wanted to change the world, and he was very passionate about social responsibilities."

"Was Parker passionate with you?"

"I've answered enough questions. Deal the cards, please."

He could feel her withdrawing and knew it was because he was pressing her, yet he couldn't seem to make himself stop.

She sneezed again and immediately apologized.

He won a game and asked, "What was it like for you in the orphanage?"

"It was nice, very nice. The sisters treated us as though we were their very own children. They were strict, like I imagine parents would be, but loving too."

"Didn't you get lonely?"

"Not very often. I had Parker to tell my secrets to when we were children. I was fortunate, and so were you because you found a family."

"Yes, I was" he agreed.

About an hour later, he finally won another game.

"Wasn't it difficult marrying your best friend?"

"Oh, no," she answered. "It was very nice. My husband was a wonderful man with many fine qualities. Why, there wasn't anything he couldn't do."

Did she really believe that nonsense? From the look on her face, he thought she did, and so he didn't contradict her. In his opinion, there wasn't anything Parker *could* do.

"Yeah, I know. The man was a saint."

Her chin came up a notch. "He was my dearest friend."

"Which means there wasn't any passion in your bed, was there?"

"You have no business asking me such personal questions."

She was right about that, he told himself, yet it didn't stop him from trying to find out everything he could about her. "What are you afraid of, Isabel? Being honest about your late husband doesn't make you a traitor. We both know it had to have been awkward making love to your best friend."

"Are you suggesting you can't be friends with your mate?"

"No," he replied. "But there has to be another element involved besides friendship."

"What element?"

He leaned forward. "Magic."

She shook her head. "I don't wish to discuss this topic any longer. It's rude of you to try to guess what my marriage was like. You never met Parker."

"I wasn't guessing," he argued. "I've already figured it all out."

"Is that so? How did you manage to do that?"

The sarcasm in her voice irritated him. "It was easy," he snapped. "The way you respond to me . . . it's all new to you, isn't it? I can see it in your every reaction. You're actually frightened by what's happening to you."

Her hands were balled into fists. "Oh? What exactly is happening to me? I'm sure you're just dying to tell me."

He leaned over the table toward her. In a low whisper he said, "I'm what's happening to you, sugar."

She bounded to her feet. "I'm going to bed. It's late."

"Don't you mean it's time for you to run and hide from me?"

"No, that isn't what I mean to say."

She took her time strolling into the bedroom. She wanted to run.

Eight

❧

$\mathcal{P}$arker wasn't putting on weight as rapidly as Douglas had hoped he would. The baby was almost six weeks old, but he still seemed to be as tiny as the day he was born. Isabel disagreed and insisted that her son had gained quite a bit of weight. Parker seemed healthy enough for his size, and he certainly had a good appetite. Dr. Simpson was the expert, and he had ordered that Parker be kept inside the cabin for a minimum of eight weeks. Douglas didn't know why the physician had settled on that specific length of time, but Douglas was going to adhere to the number no matter how anxious he was to leave.

If Parker continued to do well, he and his mother could travel in a little over fourteen days. Douglas hoped to God the weather improved before then. The rain had let up, but it was still cold and damp, and anyone who hadn't kept track of the seasons would have thought it was the middle of autumn. The night air was cold enough to require heavy flannel shirts, and Douglas was worried about keeping Parker warm when he was taken outside. Would the night air be too harsh for him to breathe?

The baby wasn't the only one he was worried about. Honest to Pete, he didn't know how he was going to last another two weeks without touching Isabel. Being in the same room with her was all it took to get him bothered. Her scent was so damned appealing, and her skin was so soft and smooth, all he wanted to think about was taking her into his arms and stroking her.

He was determined not to give in to his natural inclinations. He didn't want any complication in his life, and if he kept busy every waking hour, he was sure he'd be too tired to think about her.

After he finished up the chores in the barn around dawn, he went inside the cabin and found Isabel sitting at the table with her head in her hands. Her hair was tousled; her eyes were bleary, and her nose was bright red. She looked hungover.

"Did Parker keep you up all night?"

She sneezed before she answered. "No, I caught a little cold," she said, and promptly sneezed again.

"Maybe you should go back to bed."

She wouldn't hear of it. She had never coddled herself before, and she wasn't about to start now. After doing the washing and ironing, she cooked supper, but she couldn't eat any of it, so she fixed herself a pot of tea before she headed to bed.

She had changed into her nightgown and robe and had wrapped around her shoulders an old tattered blanket that dragged on the floor behind her. She tripped over the hem and would have dropped the tray if he hadn't grabbed it from her.

"I'll bring it in," he said. "You should probably eat something, shouldn't you? What about some toast?"

Didn't that man know how to fix anything else?

"Will you try not to burn it?" she said, trying not to sound surly.

He nodded. "You probably got sick because you work too hard."

"It's just a cold. I hope to heaven Parker doesn't catch it. What will we do if he gets a fever?"

He didn't want to think about the possibility. Parker couldn't afford to stop eating the way Isabel had.

"We'll deal with it," he assured her.

When he came back with the tray, she was just drifting off to sleep. She opened her eyes as he was turning to leave. "I'm awake."

He put the tray on the dresser, propped pillows behind her back, and then moved the tray to her lap.

He'd burned the toast again. He'd also put a white rose on the tray next to her mismatched teacup and saucer. The rose was such a sweet touch her mood improved, and she didn't mind eating the blackened bread at all.

"Is your throat sore?" he whispered.

"No. Please stop worrying."

"Isabel, I want to worry, all right? I'm good at it."

She patted the bed, waited for him to sit, and then picked up the rose. "You may be a worrier, but you're also a romantic at heart."

He shook his head and continued to frown at her. Still, his concern was unreasonable, given the fact that she was only suffering from a stuffy head.

She reached up and stroked his cheek, loving the feel of his rough skin. He hadn't shaved this morning, and the dark growth of whiskers made him look even more ruggedly handsome and somewhat dangerous.

She remembered how afraid she'd been that dark, rainy night when they met. Silhouetted against the lightning with the rising wind howling around him and the huge beast of a horse with wild eyes beside him, he was a terrifying sight. She had been certain he was going to kill her . . . until he gave the rifle back to her. She should have realized before then that he would never harm her. The gentle tone of his voice when he turned to calm the animal was one indication. The way he so carefully lifted her into his arms was certainly another. His eyes, filled with such compassion and . . .

"Isabel, you look like hell. Stop daydreaming and drink your tea before it gets cold."

She was jarred back to the present by his brisk order. "Has anyone ever told you how bossy you are, Douglas?"

"No."

"Then let me be the first. You're very bossy. Do you remember the night we met?"

The question was laughable. He shuddered every time he thought about it. "I'll never forget it."

The scowl on his face made her smile. "It wasn't that terrible."

"Yeah, it was."

"Was I difficult?"

"Oh, yes."

"I couldn't have been any worse than any of the other women you helped. I wasn't, was I?"

"I've helped lots of . . . females."

"Yes?"

He shrugged. "Yes, what?"

"Was I more difficult than the others?"

"Definitely."

"How?" she demanded.

"The others didn't try to strangle me."

"I didn't—"

"Yes, you did."

"What else did I do? It's all right. You can tell me. I promise I won't get mad." She picked up the teacup and saucer and took a long sip. "I'm waiting."

"I remember you accused me of a lot of crimes."

The glint in his eyes made it difficult for her to tell if he was being honest or not.

"Such as?"

"Let's see," he drawled out. "There were so many it's hard to keep them straight. Oh, yeah, I remember. You blamed me for getting you pregnant."

The teacup rattled in the saucer. "I didn't," she whispered.

"Yes, you did. You almost had me convinced too. Hell, I apologized," he added with a grin. "I wasn't responsible though. Trust me, sugar. I would have remembered taking you to bed."

Her blush was as red as her nose. She put the cup down on the tray but kept her attention centered on Douglas. He could tell she was trying hard not to laugh.

"What else did I accuse you of?"

"Being responsible for your agony."

"You already mentioned that one."

"Sorry. It's just kind of hard to get past it."

"Please try."

"Let's see. I was also responsible for the rain, and, oh, yeah, this one's a doozy. It was my fault you had an unhappy childhood."

"I didn't have an unhappy childhood."

"Could have fooled me. I apologized."

She burst into laughter. "You do love to exaggerate, don't you? I'm certain the other women you helped were just as difficult."

"No, they weren't."

"Who were these women? Saints?"

He moved the tray to the side table as a precautionary measure before he answered. "They weren't exactly women, at least not the way you're thinking. . . ."

She stopped smiling. "Then what were they?"

"Horses."

Her mouth dropped open. Much to his relief, she

didn't become angry. She laughed instead. "Oh, Lord, you must have been as terrified as I was."

"Yes."

"Did you have any idea what to do?"

He grinned. "Not really."

She laughed until tears came into her eyes, then realized the noise would wake Parker and quickly covered her mouth with her hand. "You were so . . . calm . . . and . . . reassuring about it all."

"I was scared."

"You?"

"Yes, me. You got real mean. That was even scarier."

"No, I didn't. Quit teasing me. I remember exactly what happened. I was in control at all times. I do recall raising my voice once or twice so you could hear me in the other room, but other than that, labor wasn't bad at all."

"Isabel, are we talking about childbirth or a tea party you attended?"

"I've never been to a tea party, but I have given birth, and I want you to know that my little aches and pains were insignificant compared to the beautiful gift I received. He's wonderful."

"Who's wonderful?"

She was exasperated. "My son. Who did you think I was talking about?"

"Me."

She would have laughed again if she hadn't started sneezing. He handed her a fresh handkerchief, told her to rest, and finally left her alone so she could.

Much to his relief, she got better in a couple of days, and thus far, Parker still hadn't caught her cold. By late Monday afternoon, Douglas was exhausted. He was drifting off to sleep in the rocker with Parker cradled in his arms when he heard the distinct sound of horses approaching. Isabel was fixing supper. She had spotted the unwanted visitors at the same time that he had heard them, for they met by the table on their way to alert one another. She reached for her son and hurried to get ready.

Douglas went to the window to check their progress. He muttered every blasphemy he could think of while he watched Boyle and a stranger who he assumed was one of the hired men coming across the yard. Douglas made up his mind to personally greet the two men. No way in hell was he going to let Isabel go outside. The terror tactics were going to stop. He actually smiled as he reached for the doorknob.

She watched him draw his weapon. She didn't have to be a mind reader to know what he was planning to do. There wasn't time to say a prayer for the sin she was going to commit. "Douglas, we're going to have to let Boyle wait. You need to look at Parker. I think he has a fever. Let Boyle wait," she repeated in a much more forceful voice.

She waited until Douglas had bolted the door and gone rushing past her, and then she asked for God's forgiveness as she picked up the rifle and ran to greet Boyle. She had to get outside before Douglas realized she'd tricked him. He was going to be furious.

Boyle was just raising his gun to fire in the air when she stepped outside. She kept one hand behind her back on the doorknob, holding it closed, and propped the rifle under her arm. Her finger was on the trigger.

"What do you want?" she demanded.

Boyle grinned at her. Isabel could barely stomach the sight. The stranger sitting atop a black mount sneered at her. She couldn't see his eyes because the brim of his hat was pulled down low over his brow, but she could feel his gaze boring into her. Like Boyle, the stranger apparently didn't consider the rifle much of a threat. He had both hands stacked on top of his pommel.

"You ain't being very sociable, Isabel, pointing your rifle at me."

"Get off my land, Boyle."

"I'll go when I'm ready. I came here to tell you I'm going to be away for a spell. Don't go getting your hopes up 'cause I'm coming back. I'm going to my annual family get-together, and I expect I'll be away a good six weeks, maybe even longer. Now, I don't want you feeling lonely while I'm gone, so I'm putting my right-hand man in charge of you. His name is Spear."

He turned to his cohort, told him to tip his hat to his future bride, and then turned back to Isabel.

"Spear's going to watch out for you. I've put some of my men up on the mountain yonder to watch over you too. They'll be staying day and night. Are you comforted by my thoughtfulness? I wouldn't want you to think you had to leave while I was gone. Next year you'll be going with me. You understand what I'm saying, girl?"

The mockery in his voice infuriated her. "Go away," she shouted.

He laughed. "I expect you will have had that thing by the time I get back. Your figure should be nice and curvy again by the time we get married. Are you about ready to accept your future, honey bell, and start begging me?"

She answered him by cocking her rifle. Spear's hand went to his gun, but he didn't draw.

Boyle jerked on his reins and rode away. Spear followed. "Didn't I tell you she was full of spit and vinegar?" Boyle shouted. "She'll beg me though, and she'll do it in front of the entire town. Just you wait and see."

Isabel didn't hear Spear's answer. Boyle's laughter drowned it out. She stood there on the stoop for several minutes, watching them leave . . . and gathering the gumption to face Douglas again.

She considered staying where she was for the rest of the day, but Douglas had other ideas. She didn't hear the door open. She did feel herself being pulled backward though, and the grip on her waist, even with the padding, felt like a vice. Fortunately, she had enough presence of mind to put the safety on the rifle before she dropped it.

He caught it before it hit the floor, kicked the door closed, and turned her around to face him before he let go of her.

The padding around her waist dropped to the floor, and she kicked it out of the way. She had already determined the strategy she would employ. From the look in his eyes, she knew he wasn't going to be reasonable, and since her only defense was to retreat or attack, she chose the latter.

She took a step forward, planted her hands on her hips, and frowned up at him.

"You listen to me, Mr. Clayborne. If you had gone outside, you would have tried to shoot both of them, and one of them might have killed you. And just where would Parker and I be then, I ask you? Boyle has friends, remember? If you'd killed him, they'd come looking for him, and we would have to fight twenty-some men off while trying to protect an infant. I'm a good shot, and I imagine you are too, but I'm also a realist, and there's no way we could get all of them before we were killed. Am I getting through to you yet?"

She guessed she wasn't when he spoke. "If he comes here again, you aren't going outside to talk to him."

"I knew you'd be stubborn about this."

"You lied to me, and I want you to promise me you'll never do it again."

"Now you've done it. You woke the baby. You go get him."

"Neither one of us is moving until I get your promise. You have any idea how scared I got when I thought Parker was sick? Damn it, Isabel, if you ever lie to me . . ."

"If it meant saving your hide, I'd lie again. We

should be celebrating now, not bickering. Didn't you hear what Boyle said? He's finally leaving. That's wonderful news."

"I'm waiting."

"Oh, all right. I promise never to lie to you again. Now, if you'll excuse me, I'll go to my son."

"I'll get him."

All Parker needed was a dry bottom, and as soon as Douglas changed him, the baby went back to sleep.

Douglas couldn't get Spear off his mind. From the look of him, Douglas knew he was going to be a much more dangerous threat than Boyle could ever be.

Isabel noticed how quiet he was during supper and asked him to tell her what he was thinking about.

"Spear," he answered. "Boyle doesn't worry me nearly as much as his new hired hand does."

"I disagree. Boyle's cruel and heartless."

"He's also a coward."

"How do you know that?"

"He preys on women, that's how I know. He isn't going to be a problem to get rid of now that I know what his biggest flaw is."

"He has at least a hundred flaws, but you still can't kill him. You'd spend the rest of your life in prison . . . or hang, God forbid."

"I won't kill him. I've thought of something worse. I'm kind of looking forward to his day of reckoning too."

"What are you going to do?"

"Wait and see."

"Is it legal?"

He shrugged, then said, "I wonder if Boyle has hired any other new men."

"Do you mean like Spear?"

He nodded. "Since Boyle was nice enough to let us know he has men watching the ranch, I'm going to ride up in the hills every night and listen in on their conversation for a little while."

"Is that necessary?

"Yes, it's necessary," he insisted. "Parker's going to be eight weeks old soon and Dr. Simpson said he would be strong enough to move."

"He also said ten weeks would be better."

"Is Parker putting on any weight?"

"Of course he is."

Douglas wasn't convinced. "Every time I pick him up, I realize how fragile and tiny he is. He doesn't feel any heavier to me."

"Do you forget how big you are? No wonder he doesn't feel heavier to you. He is getting stronger every day, but it's still too soon to take him out in the cold night air."

"We might have to chance it," he argued.

"I won't put him in jeopardy."

"And staying here isn't doing just that?"

"I really don't want to talk about this now."

"Too bad," he snapped. "We're going to talk about it. You have to listen to reason. My brothers will help protect you and Parker, and it's best if we leave while Boyle's away. I'll make sure he really left town before . . ."

She was vehemently shaking her head. "Parker's too little to be taken out."

"If the doctor thinks we should risk it, will you be reasonable then?"

She had to think about it for a long while before she finally agreed. "As long as you don't change his mind for him. Don't try to talk him into it, Douglas."

He agreed with a nod. "Do you have any idea what you want to do when you leave here?"

She still hadn't made up her mind about the future. She could either move back to Chicago and teach at the orphanage or stay in Sweet Creek and secure a teaching position in town or in nearby Liddyville.

The future didn't frighten her. It was leaving the past behind that made her ache so. She was a realist and she knew she had to leave the ranch because of the dangerous spot where her late husband had insisted their home be built. Eventually the flood waters would wash the cabin away. Yes, she knew she had to leave, yet the idea of packing up and walking away made her feel like such a failure. The land and the home were the fulfillment of Parker's dream. He had died protecting it, and, God help her, where was she going to get the strength to leave his dream behind?

Douglas wouldn't understand the anguish she felt, and she didn't want to explain it.

"I don't want to discuss it now."

"You're going to have to face the future sooner or later."

She got up from the table and hurried into the kitchen. "I have time to decide, now that Boyle's leaving."

"No, you don't have time, unless you've lost your mind and believe anything that bastard tells you."

"Do you like cake? I thought I'd bake one and you could have some when you get back from town."

"For the love of God, you've got to face facts, not bake."

She pushed the curtain back so she could see him. "I want to bake now." Each word was said in a slow, precise monotone. "I work problems out in my mind when I bake. Do you like cake or not?"

She looked mad enough to shoot him if he told her no. He gave up trying to make her be reasonable. "Sure."

Douglas left the ranch a few minutes later. He checked on Boyle's lookouts before he headed into town and didn't arrive at Simpson's house until midnight.

The doctor was waiting at the kitchen table with a steaming cup of coffee in one hand and his pistol in the other.

"You're late tonight," he remarked. "Sit down and I'll get you some coffee, son. How's the baby doing?"

Douglas pulled out the chair, straddled it, and told the doctor not to bother with coffee.

"Parker's doing all right, but Isabel's recovering from a cold. What should we do if the baby catches it?"

"Keep him warm. . . ."

"We've been keeping him warm. Isn't there anything else we can do? What if he gets a fever?"

"Douglas, it won't do any good to snap at me. The baby's too small for medicine. We just have to hope and pray he doesn't get sick."

"I want to get them both out of that death trap she calls home. If I'm real careful, couldn't I . . ."

He stopped trying to plead his case when Simpson shook his head at him.

"It's a miracle that baby's surviving, and that's a fact, coming early the way he did. Do you realize how you'd be tempting fate by taking him out at night? And where are you thinking you'll take them? Boyle will turn Sweet Creek upside down searching for them, and you don't dare risk going to Liddyville because you won't know who Boyle has in his hip pocket. I know we've been over this before. Boyle's got friends in Liddyville too, and someone will hear about your arrival. Folks gossip with one another. I'm telling you, it's too dangerous."

Douglas could feel a pounding headache coming on. "What a mess," he muttered.

"Is Isabel anxious to leave?"

He shook his head. "She knows she has to, but she won't talk about her future yet. She keeps putting it off. It's damned frustrating."

"I know it is. I've got some more bad news for you," Simpson said. "Boyle went and hired himself a new man. He goes by the name of Spear, and he's got a real mean look about him. I nosed around to find out what I could and heard that Boyle met Spear when he was on one of his annual trips back to family in the Dakotas. By the way, Boyle's leaving tomorrow morning. I heard him telling Jasper Cooper he was putting Spear in charge while he's gone." The doctor took a drink of his coffee, and then said, "No one in town suspects Isabel's gotten help. Time's on your side because you've got at least another month to fatten that baby up and get him thriving before Boyle comes back."

"You told me the baby could be moved when he was eight weeks old."

"I also told you ten would be better."

"If I could bring help in now, couldn't—"

"Think it through, son. You don't want to put Isabel and her son in the middle of a war, do you? No, of course you don't. Look on the bright side," he suggested. He ignored Douglas's incredulous look and continued on. "You've done fine for over seven weeks now, and I'm sure you can hold out a little longer without any trouble at all. Then you can send for help and get Isabel and her son out of there. I still don't cotton to the notion of taking that baby out at night, but the more weight he has on him, the better his chances will be. With Boyle away, it should get easier. Do you see? It isn't all grim, is it?"

"Hell, yes, it is."

Simpson chuckled. "She's getting to you, isn't she, son?"

Douglas shrugged but didn't say a word.

"I can see it plain as day. Are you thinking about falling in love with our girl?"

"No." He gave the denial with passion and conviction.

It wasn't a lie because he wasn't "thinking" about it. He already was in love with her.

Nine

❦

$\mathcal{D}$ouglas's life was miserable. He had never experienced such acute frustration before, and needless to say, he didn't like it at all. He was also angry with Isabel most of the time. Fortunately, she didn't know how he felt, and he was certain she didn't notice how he stared at her whenever she was in the room. The doctor was right when he'd told Douglas that she was too pretty for her own good.

He tried to stay away from her as much as possible. He vowed to stop trying to get her to acknowledge the physical attraction between them. It was wrong to do so and he knew it. Besides, it was apparent that she wasn't ready to admit that her marriage had been less than satisfactory or that Parker had had a few glaring inadequacies. If she was determined to elevate the man to sainthood, that was just fine with Douglas. From now on, no matter how ignorant, incompetent, and foolish he personally believed the man had been, he would keep his opinion to himself. What right did he have to criticize the dead anyway? And why did it bother him that she was so devoted to Parker's memory?

Because she obviously still loved Parker.

Douglas recognized he wasn't being logical. The issue bothering him was loyalty. He had always liked people who proved they were loyal, especially when it wasn't easy. They were several notches above everyone else in character. Like his family . . . and Isabel. Yes, Isabel. She continued to be loyal to her dead husband, and the truth was, Douglas didn't expect less from her. Still, did she have to be so blindly loyal? She had given Parker her faith, her love, and her undying loyalty, and he had failed on all counts.

It wasn't going to matter to Douglas any longer. Just as soon as the baby put on a little more weight, he would get the two of them out of Sweet Creek, take care of Boyle and his hired gunslingers, and then go back home, where he belonged. Until that day arrived, he planned to be polite but distant with Isabel.

That was easier said than done.

The days were unbearable, for as soon as he fell asleep, his mind was filled with erotic dreams about her. He couldn't control his thoughts when he was at rest, and he soon got to the point where he dreaded closing his eyes.

She'd made it worse for him by demanding that he stop sleeping on his bedroll and use her bed. She had a valid argument. She was awake during the day, and if he moved little Parker's bed into the outer room, Douglas could sleep without interruption.

The problem wasn't the noise. He didn't want to be surrounded by her light, feminine scent, but he'd go to his death before he told her so. She wouldn't understand anyway, and because he didn't want to hurt her feelings, he tossed and turned, gritted his teeth, and wondered how much torture a man could take before he snapped.

The baby was the only joy in his life. Parker was slowly putting on weight and seemed to be getting stronger with each passing day. Although it didn't seem possible, he grew louder as well. Douglas didn't think infants developed personalities until they were much older, around five or six months, but Isabel's son proved to be as extraordinary as his sister, Mary Rose, when she'd been a baby.

Parker was thinner than Mary Rose, but he was still able to exert his power over both adults by simply opening his mouth and screaming for service.

Douglas had given his heart to the little tyrant. Admittedly there were times when he was pacing back and forth in the middle of the night with the baby up against his shoulder that he wanted to pack cotton in his ears just to get a moment of blissful silence. Yet there were also times when Parker had his fist wrapped around one of Douglas's fingers, gripping it tight. Douglas would look down at the baby sleeping so peacefully in his arms and feel the tremendous bond that had formed between them. He had helped bring Parker into the world and, like a father, he longed to watch him grow.

Oh, yes, Parker was a joy to be around. His mother wasn't. The physical attraction to her kept getting stronger, and though he tried to convince himself that she was untouchable, the pretense didn't work. After living together so intimately for eight weeks, the tension and frustration had become palpable.

Isabel had a different point of view. She was certain Douglas couldn't wait to be rid of her. He could barely stomach being in the same room with her, and no matter how she tried to get his attention, he blatantly ignored her. If she accidentally touched his arm, or not so accidentally moved closer to him, he became tense and out of sorts.

His attitude upset her more than she wanted to admit. Heaven help her, she was even having indecent dreams about him, and in every single one of them, she was always the aggressor. She couldn't understand why she wasn't dreaming about her late husband. She should be, shouldn't she? Parker had been her dearest friend. Douglas was a friend too, but he was the complete opposite of her husband, for while Parker had been sweet and gentle but somewhat impractical, Douglas was passionate, sexy, incredibly virile, and practical about everything from childbirth to politics. He was filled with confidence, and for the first time in her life, she felt as though she had someone who could, and would, do his part. Until Douglas had come along, she had carried the burden alone.

She wanted him in a way she had never wanted her husband, and that was painfully difficult for her to admit. Mating with her husband had been a necessary duty to produce a child, which both Isabel and Parker wanted, but neither one of them joined together with any enthusiasm. She had been overjoyed to realize she was pregnant, but she'd also been relieved. After Dr. Simpson confirmed the diagnosis, neither she nor her husband ever again reached for the other during the night.

Isabel ached over the loss of her dear friend, but she didn't miss what she had never experienced . . . until Douglas came into her life.

She wanted to dislike him just to stop herself from having such inappropriate daydreams about him, yet she also dreaded their eventual separation.

She wasn't the only one filled with confusion. She was certain she was confusing God as well. She prayed that Douglas would leave. She prayed that he would stay. Hopefully, God would be able to sort it all out.

Late one afternoon Douglas caught her bathing. She had assumed he was sound asleep, since the bedroom door was closed and she'd been as quiet as a mouse while she filled the metal tub with water she'd heated over the flames in the hearth. She didn't want to awaken him, so she had eased into the water and washed every inch of her body without making a single splash or once sighing out loud. She had just retied the ribbon holding her hair atop her head, leaned back, and closed her eyes, when she heard the telltale groan of a floorboard.

She opened her eyes just as Douglas walked out of the bedroom.

They both froze. Too stunned to speak, she could only stare up at him in true astonishment. He looked thunderstruck, making it more than apparent he hadn't expected to find her stripped bare, sitting in a tub of water with her shoulders and toes peeking out at him.

He didn't have all his clothes on. She noticed right away. His legs were braced apart. He was barefoot and wore only a pair of snug buckskin pants he hadn't bothered to button. Dark curly hair covered his chest, and when her gaze began to move lower, she forced herself to close her eyes.

She finally found her voice. "You forgot to button your pants, for heaven's sake."

She had to be joking. He wasn't stark naked; she was. He didn't look at her for more than a second or two, but it was still long enough for him to see golden shoulders, pink toes, and damn near everything in between.

Ah, hell, she had a sprinkle of freckles on her breasts.

He got even with her for her inadvertent torture the only way he could. He turned around, stomped back into the bedroom, and slammed the door behind him.

The noise awakened the baby, infuriating her. She

was suddenly so angry with Douglas, there wasn't room for embarrassment, and if she hadn't regained her wits in the nick of time, she would have chased after him wrapped in only a thin towel so that she could tell him she was sick and tired of being treated like a leper.

The baby had other ideas. By the time she dried herself off and put her robe on, he had worked himself into a rage. He was tearing at his mouth with his tiny fists while he screamed for his milk. The drawer was on the table, and as she lifted him into her arms, her anger intensified. Her sweet baby shouldn't have to sleep in a dresser drawer for the love of God, and just why hadn't Douglas done something about it?

After she had changed Parker's diaper and gown, she sat in the rocker and fed him. She whispered to him all about Douglas's transgressions. Parker's eyes were open, and he stared up at her until he had taken his fill. Before she'd even moved him to her shoulder, he let out a loud belch, closed his eyes, and went back to sleep.

She held him in one arm and rocked him until she got dizzy and realized how fast she was going.

Douglas came out a minute later. She didn't dare speak to him while she was so angry. She needed to calm down first.

She handed the baby to him without bothering to look up, changed the bedding in the drawer, then reclaimed her son and put him down for the night.

Supper was almost ready. She'd made a big iron kettle of thick stew and only needed to move the drawer, set the table and warm the biscuits.

He didn't stay inside long enough to eat. He told her he had chores to do, and left. She knew he was as angry with her as she was with him, but he wouldn't lose his temper no matter how much or how often he was provoked, and if that wasn't the most frustrating trait in a man, she didn't know what was. Did he have to be so stoic all the time? Come to think of it, he never ever lost his control, and that simply wasn't human, was it?

He exhibited amazing restraint. The longer she thought about that horrible flaw, the angrier she became. Then she burned the biscuits, and, honest to heaven, that was the last straw. He was going to eat them anyway, she vowed, even if she had to force them down his throat. He was also going to eat the stew she'd spent hours preparing.

Isabel knew she wasn't being reasonable. It didn't seem to matter. It felt good to be angry and frustrated and know that she could blow up at him and still remain perfectly safe. Yes, safe. He made her feel safe, and so gloriously alive, even when he was acting like a bad-tempered boar.

She decided to behave like an adult. She would take his supper to him in the barn as a peace offering. That act of thoughtfulness would surely get him out of his contrary mood. After he'd eaten, she would demand that he tell her what was bothering him and why he'd become so impossible to live with lately. If he wanted specifics, she had plenty.

She checked on Parker one last time, tied her hair back with a white ribbon, and then carried the tray to the barn. She practiced what she would say to him on the way. "I was sure you would be hungry by now, and so I . . ."

No, she could do better than that. She wanted to sound blasé, not timid.

"I'll leave the tray by the door, Douglas. If you get hungry, help yourself," she whispered. Yes, that was better, much better. Then she would suggest they sit down and talk when he was finished.

She straightened her shoulders and went inside. She spotted Douglas at the opposite end of the barn. He had his sleeves rolled up and was pouring a large bucket of water into a metal vat. Two empty buckets were on the floor next to him. He straightened up, rolled his shoulders to work the stiffness out, brushed his hands off on a towel he'd draped over a post, and went to Pegasus's stall.

She walked forward so she could see the stallion. She could hear Douglas whispering to the animal, but she couldn't hear what he was saying. She saw him stroke the stallion's neck, and Pegasus was letting him know how much he liked the attention by nuzzling Douglas's shoulder.

He knew she was there watching him. He'd have to be dead and buried not to hear all the racket she was making. She'd talked herself into the barn and was now obviously having difficulty holding on to the tray. She was either nervous or making the noise on purpose to get him to notice her. The glass was banging against the plate, and out of the corner of his eye, he could see the utensils bouncing up and down.

He wanted to get past his irritation before he spoke to her. If he so much as looked at her now, he knew he'd lose his temper, hurt her tender feelings, and then feel rotten about it.

"Douglas, how long are you going to ignore me?"

He finally turned around. "I thought I'd try to figure out why you broke your promise to me. You remember, don't you? I'm sure I asked you to give me your word that you would stay inside at night because I can't keep watch over you and be in the barn at the same time."

She put the tray down on the seat of the buggy to her right before answering him.

"Yes, I remember, but I thought you might be hungry, and I—"

He deliberately interrupted her. "Do you also remember why we thought it might be dangerous?"

"Douglas, you don't have to treat me like a child. I know exactly what I promised. I know why you were so insistent too. I told you that once . . . just once, some of Boyle's men got all liquored up and rode down the hill during the night, and that was when you suggested I stay inside."

"You left something out."

"I did?"

He gave her a look that let her know he didn't believe she'd forgotten. "You told me they tried to break into the cabin. Remember?"

She knew he was right. She shouldn't have taken the risk. She should have stayed inside the cabin with her son. It was her duty to protect him. Oh, Lord, the Winchester! She'd left the rifle inside by the window.

"I wasn't thinking. There, are you happy? I admitted it. I've been preoccupied lately. Now, if you'll excuse me, I'll go back to my son."

She turned around and hurried out of the barn. "Isabel, where's the rifle?"

She didn't answer. He knew good and well where it was, since she hadn't had it in her hands when she'd come into the barn. He'd asked the question just to make her feel like an idiot. She certainly felt like one, and that made her angry with herself. If she hadn't been so distracted by Douglas, she would never have done such a foolish thing.

Douglas strode past her and checked on Parker. The baby was sleeping soundly in the drawer on the table. He would have moved him back to the bedroom, but his hands were greasy, and he decided to wait until he had washed first. Isabel stood by his side, looking down at her son. Douglas didn't say another word to her. The two of them were past due for a long discussion about her future, he decided, and just as soon as he had cleaned up, he planned to sit her down and force her to make a few decisions.

He grabbed a thick, clean towel, a bar of soap, and headed back to the barn to take a bath.

He scrubbed the dirt from his body, but the cold

water didn't rid him of the fever he'd felt for weeks now, every time he thought about Isabel. Unfortunately, that was most of the days and nights. No, cold water didn't help. He could have washed in snow and still burned inside to touch her.

He needed to get away from her as soon as possible, but he couldn't do that until she told him where, in God's name, she wanted to go. She had procrastinated as long as he was going to allow. Before the night was over, she was going to make a decision. Douglas knew he needed to get a grip on himself. He knew how too. All he had to do was get the hell away from Isabel, because she was turning him into a raving animal.

Things were going to change from this moment on. He put on clean clothes, turned down the lantern light, and went to have the long overdue talk with Isabel.

She was waiting for him.

He took the tray with the untouched supper to the kitchen. "We need to talk," he whispered so he wouldn't disturb the baby. "First, I'll put Parker away."

"Back in the dresser?" Her voice was brittle.

"This isn't the time to get into one of your moods, Isabel. We need to . . ."

"One of my moods? I can't believe you just said . . . Leave the drawer on the table and come with me. I want you to see something."

She hurried into the bedroom so he wouldn't argue with her. As soon as he came inside, she shut the door and then dramatically pointed to the bedroll on the floor next to her bed.

"Would you mind explaining why you slept on the floor today when there was a perfectly good bed a foot away? I think I know why, but I want to hear you tell me anyway."

"Why do you think I slept on the floor?" he hedged.

"Because the thought of getting into my bed was so repulsive you chose the hard floor instead. I'm right, aren't I?"

"No, you aren't."

He had the gall to scowl, and that infuriated her.

She moved to the other side of the bed to put some distance between them. "You don't have to deny it. I know you don't like being here. You can barely stand to be in the same room with me. What did I do to make you feel this way, Douglas? No, don't answer that. I think the time has come for you to leave. That's what you were going to talk about, wasn't it?"

He couldn't believe a woman could be this naive. She'd twisted everything around, and, honest to God, he couldn't figure out how she had come up with such outrageous conclusions. Hadn't anyone ever told her how pretty she was?

"You really don't have any idea what I'm thinking, do you?" He was astonished by the revelation.

She took a deep breath, ordered herself to stop criticizing him, and then apologized. "I'm sorry I snapped at you. If it weren't for you, I don't know what Parker and I would have done. I felt so powerless then. I should be thanking you for your help, and my only excuse for acting like a shrew is that I haven't been feeling myself lately."

"Why is that?"

"Why? Take a look around, Douglas. My life is in shambles. I don't know how—"

"Now, Isabel, it isn't that bleak."

He was going to remind her she had a handsome son who was getting stronger every day, but she didn't give him time to get another word in.

She wasn't in the mood to be reasonable and didn't particularly like being contradicted. Her voice became shrill when she continued on.

"Of course it's bleak. My son is sleeping in a dresser drawer, for God's sake, when he should have a proper cradle, and I shouldn't have to be terrified every time it rains. Don't you think I know where Parker had the cabin built? Everyone in town tried to talk him out of it, but he was determined to prove them wrong. There, are you happy? I've admitted he wasn't perfect. Neither are you, Douglas. You're rude and cold and so horribly reasonable all the time you make me want to scream."

"You are screaming, sugar."

"Don't you dare start being sweet. Don't you ever lose your composure?"

"Is it my turn yet? You keep asking me questions, but you don't let me answer them."

He sounded cool and collected, as always. It drove her to distraction. "Don't you have any idea how much you frustrate me?"

"You want to talk about frustration?" He let out a harsh laugh and came toward her. "You're looking at it, Isabel. You've got to be blind or just plain nuts not to know what the mere sight of you does to me."

Once he got started, the words poured out and he couldn't make himself stop.

"I sleep on the floor because your scent is on the sheets, woman, and it makes me so damned hot I can't sleep. All I want to think about is making love to you. Now do you understand?"

He was suddenly pressing her up against the wall and glaring down at her. "Are you getting scared yet? Or have I stunned you speechless by shocking your sensibilities? What the hell are you smiling about, Isabel? I want to take you to bed. Got that? Now aren't you frightened?"

She slowly shook her head. "Isabel, I'm begging you. Tell me to leave."

"Stay."

"Do you understand . . ."

"Oh, yes, I understand," she whispered.

She threw her arms around his neck.

He gently cupped the sides of her face and slowly leaned down. "I tried to stay away from you. . . ."

"You did?" she asked with a long, breathless sigh.

"I wasn't strong enough to resist you. It was those sexy . . ."

"Freckles?"

"Yeah, freckles. A man can only take so much temptation before he's got to take a bite out of the apple, sugar, and when I saw you bathing, I . . ."

"Douglas, are you ever going to kiss me?"

She had barely gotten her question out before his mouth came down on hers. It wasn't perfect; it was much, much better. Her reaction was instantaneous. Her entire body responded to his kiss, and when his tongue brushed against hers, she imitated his action and kissed him with all the pent-up passion inside her.

He kept her glued against him while he continued to try to devour her. It would be over before he'd even begun to do all the things he wanted to do if he didn't get her to slow down, yet the thought of stopping so he could explain was simply too much for him to accept.

Neither one of them remembered undressing the other or getting into bed. Douglas thought he might have thrown her there in his haste to cover her with his body. Then again, she might have thrown him down. She seemed to have acquired an amazing amount of strength in the past few minutes as she forced him to let her kiss every inch of his chest.

He didn't give her any resistance. Dear God, how he loved her. She was everything he had ever wanted in a lover.

The feel of her warm skin against his own was incredibly arousing. She was so perfect everywhere. He loved the way her breasts fell against his chest, and the way she gasped each time he moved against her drove him wild. She didn't try to conceal the fact that she was as hot for him as he was for her, and so he let go of his control and his inhibitions.

He kissed her neck, her shoulders, her breasts, and then slowly moved lower.

"What are you doing?" she whispered, her voice raw with passion.

"I'm kissing every freckle on your body."

She thought those were the most romantic words she'd ever heard. "Oh, my," she whispered, over and over again, each time he touched or kissed or stroked her.

He overwhelmed her senses until she was incapable of thought. She thought he asked her to tell him if he did anything she didn't like, and she really tried to answer him, to tell him that nothing he did could be wrong, but every time she tried to speak, he did something more wonderful to her, and she couldn't get more than a sigh or a whimper out.

If he meant to drive her crazy, he succeeded gloriously. When at last he finally came to her, she felt a twinge of pain as he slowly moved inside her, and then he was part of her and holding her so tenderly, and there wasn't any pain, only pleasure.

He savored each whisper, each movement, and when at last the need to find release became unbearable, he forced her fulfillment by increasing the rhythm and tightening his grip.

Ecstasy such as she had never experienced before began with a ripple, then increased within a heartbeat to an explosive climax. She clung to him as the world fragmented into a thousand brilliant stars, the wonder of their lovemaking filled with beauty and joy.

It took several minutes for him to recover. He held her close to him, nuzzling her neck and lazily stroking her.

"Are you all right?" he whispered.

She didn't answer him, but she did sigh against his

ear, and he knew, before he found enough strength to lift his head and look at her face, that she was happy.

He was arrogantly satisfied to know that he had exhausted her. She fell asleep clinging to him, her long legs entwined with his, her face nestled in the crook of his neck, and for this moment in time, she belonged completely to him.

It would have to be enough to last a lifetime.

Ten

Lying in the darkness with Isabel in his arms, Douglas was plagued with guilt. Making love to her had been a terrible mistake. He had taken advantage of her when she was most vulnerable and totally dependent on him to protect her and her son. He hadn't been honorable. What in God's name had he been thinking? Hell, he hadn't been thinking at all, at least not with his head, or he would never have reached for her. His sin was unforgivable, and yet he knew that he would never forget how she had felt in his arms. The memory of her was going to haunt him for the rest of his life.

Now he was going to hurt her by making her face reality too. Circumstance had thrown them together, but in another time and place, she would never have chosen him. When she returned to the outside world, she would realize it.

He was the complete antithesis of her late husband.

Parker had been a dreamer. Douglas was a realist, and until recently, he had also been a reasonable man.

The baby's demand for attention forced Douglas to put his grim thoughts aside. He changed Parker's diaper, and then rocked him while he explained the torment he was going through. The baby stopped fretting for several minutes and stared up at him with what Douglas interpreted as intellectual curiosity.

He felt as though he would soon lose his son. From the moment Parker had come into the world, Douglas had loved and cherished him as though he were the boy's father.

The baby was lulled back to sleep. Douglas kissed his forehead, told him in a whisper that he loved him, and put him back in bed.

He gently shook Isabel awake. She put her arms around his neck and tried to pull him down into bed with her. He kissed her brow, insisted she open her eyes, and promised she could sleep just as soon as he returned from his nightly ritual.

"Do you have to check on Boyle's men every night?"

"Yes."

She was too sleepy to argue with him. She followed him to the front door so that she could secure the lock after he'd left.

"How long will you be gone?"

"Same as usual," he answered. "I'll listen to their conversation for a little while, and then come back."

"They haven't said anything important yet," she reminded him.

"I'm still checking."

She yawned, assured him she would stay awake, and kissed him. "Be careful."

The lure of her soft body was difficult to resist. An hour later he was thankful he'd kept to his routine, for Boyle's men were in a talkative mood. As usual, they were also drunk. The topic was different tonight, because they weren't railing against Boyle for making them stay out all night. The target for their resentment was Isabel. Their anger was fully directed on her. If she weren't such a stubborn woman, she would realize how rich and powerful Boyle was and do as he ordered. Their boss wanted her to get down on her knees and beg him to marry her, and it was the unanimous opinion of the hired hands that it was only a matter of time before she did exactly that.

Douglas had heard all the complaints before, but never with such venom. Then one of the men suggested they all go along with Spear's plan to break into Isabel's home and take her over to Boyle's ranch.

"Spear's wanting to impress the boss, and he's sure that putting the woman in his bed ought to do the trick. He thinks Boyle will give him a big bonus, and if everyone goes along with the plan, he promised to share some of the money with us."

Two of the men were dead set against the plan. One harped on the fact that they hadn't been paid for the last month's work because Boyle was making them wait until he returned from the Dakotas.

It soon became apparent to Douglas that even the men who were against Spear's plan feared him. It would be only a matter of time before they became too frightened not to agree.

Hearing what the men said about Isabel infuriated Douglas, and he was only able to control his rage by forcing himself to remember that Isabel and Parker came first. When they were safe, Boyle and his men were all going to be fair game.

God, how Douglas looked forward to it.

Time had run out. Douglas made the decision to send for his brothers, and continued on to the physician's house.

As he expected, Simpson argued with him, but Douglas wouldn't listen to a word he said.

"Boyle might not be back for another week or two,

and that baby needs every extra hour you can give him before you uproot him and take him out into the wild. He's too fragile to go anywhere yet."

"Do you know what will happen if Spear comes down to the ranch? I'll kill him, and then Boyle will come running with at least twenty men. Parker won't have any chance at all if a war starts. You know I'm right. Send the damn telegram tomorrow."

"God help you, son."

In the past, Douglas had always been blunt to a fault, and when he talked to Isabel the following morning, he reverted to his old ways.

He paced in front of the hearth until she joined him. She had her sewing basket in her hands and hurried to put it on the table so she could hug him.

He told her to sit down, and still, she didn't have any inkling of what he was about to say to her until she looked at his face.

"What's wrong?"

"We're what's wrong."

Her eyes widened in disbelief. "No."

"Yes," he insisted. "I shouldn't have taken you to bed last night, and I want you to try to understand. I took advantage of you, and that was wrong. For God's sake, don't shake your head at me. You know I'm right. I could have gotten you pregnant, Isabel. It can't happen again."

She was stunned by his cruel words and the anger in his voice. "I won't understand," she cried out. "Why are you saying these things to me? Don't you realize how much you're hurting me?"

"Please don't make this any more difficult than it already is. I could give you a hundred reasons why it was wrong."

"Give me one reason that makes sense."

"You felt obligated to me."

"Of course I felt obligated to you, but that isn't why

I wanted to make love to you. Don't do this. What happened between us wasn't wrong . . . It was beautiful . . . and loving . . . and . . . " She couldn't go on. Tears gathered in her eyes as she turned away from him. Did the hours they'd shared together mean so little to him? No, she wouldn't believe that. She couldn't.

"Once you've rejoined the outside world, this interlude will—"

"Interlude?" she whispered. "For the love of God, will you stop being so practical all the time and listen to your heart?"

"Stop being practical? Damn it, woman, if I'd been practical, I would have gotten you and Parker the hell out of here a long time ago, and I would have kept my hands off of you."

"I wouldn't have left. It would have been dangerous for my son. It was prudent to stay, and last night I wanted you as much as you wanted me."

She ran to him and tried to put her arms around him. He pulled back and shook his head.

"Will you try to understand? We were thrown together by circumstances beyond our control. You were desperate, and so thankful for my help you've mistaken gratitude for love. It's a bad foundation for a lasting commitment, and with time and distance, you'll realize I'm right. You must go forward with your son, Isabel. That's the way it has to be."

"Without you?"

"Yes."

He was through discussing the matter, and she was too devastated to try to make him change his mind.

She walked toward the bedroom, praying that he would follow her and say something that would give her hope for a future with him.

He didn't say a word. She turned back to him to plead one last time, but the words became trapped in her throat. The sight of him was as heartbreaking as his harsh words had been. He was standing in front of the hearth with his head bent, his hands braced on the mantle. The lines of his face revealed the anguish within.

He looked grief-stricken. Had he just told her goodbye?

"Douglas, does it matter that I love you?"

His silence was her answer.

Eleven

Isabel and Douglas avoided each other as much as possible for the next two days. She was lost in her thoughts about a future without him and was desperately trying to accept his decision to leave her and Parker. He, on the other hand, was considering the more practical matter of keeping them all alive until help arrived.

He still hadn't told her about the plan he'd heard Boyle's men discussing, nor had he told her the wire had been sent to his brothers, but, God help him, it hadn't been for lack of trying. Each time he broached the topic, she turned away from him and walked out of the room to attend to her son.

He kept busy each day until it was dark enough for him to ride up the hills to check on Boyle's men.

She baked. By early evening of the second day, there were four pies and two cakes on the table. She was still at it when he got ready to leave.

"Could you stop stirring that dough long enough to listen to me?"

"Of course."

He realized it would be asking too much of her to request that she look at him. He knew how hurt she was, and he wondered if she had any idea how hard she was making this for him. He didn't ask her, for he had no wish to get into another discussion. If she cried again, it would kill him. His mind was made up, and he was convinced that he was doing the right thing. In time, and with distance separating them, she would understand.

"If you're not too tired by the time I get back, I think it would be a good idea for you to pack a few things to take with you when we leave."

"I'm not too tired."

"Bolt the door after me."

"No one's going to be watching the cabin tonight because of the rain."

"I'm still going to check."

"I love you, Douglas." She blurted the words out before she could stop herself. "I'm trying to understand why you would—"

He cut her off. "You're too upset to talk about this. When you can be more . . ."

"Practical?"

"Yes."

She came close to throwing the biscuit dough at him. She put the bowl down on the counter before she could act on the urge and followed him to the door.

Then she waited for him to kiss her good-bye, knowing full well that he wouldn't. As soon as the lock was latched, she burst into tears. Love wasn't supposed to be this painful, was it? How in God's name could she make him understand that what they had was real? Why was he throwing it away? She knew he loved her and that he believed with all his heart that he had acted dishonorably and taken advantage of her. He was wrong, but he was also a proud and stubborn man, and she didn't know how to change his mind. With time and distance would he come to his senses, or would he continue to believe he had done the right thing by leaving?

Please, God, don't let him leave Parker and me. Help him realize we were meant to be together.

The thought of a future without Douglas was unbearable, and within minutes she was doubled over and gasping for breath between heart-wrenching sobs.

She didn't hear Boyle's men until their horses came galloping into the yard. In less than a heartbeat, gunshots were fired and the cabin was riddled with bullets. The men were circling her home, shouting vile threats and obscenities at her while they continued to empty their guns.

Dear God, the baby . . . She had to get to her baby and protect him. She ran to him, frantic now to keep him safe. She was whimpering low in her throat as she lifted her son into her arms. She hunched over so that her body protected him and turned to an inside wall. A stray bullet would have to pass through her before it could get to him.

The noise was deafening. Gunshots were ricocheting off the walls, men were shouting, Parker was crying, and all she could think about was finding a safe place where she could hide her son.

There wasn't time to comfort Parker. He needed to be safe.

SAFE . . . Dear God, help me keep him safe . . . help me . . .

The wardrobe. Yes, the wardrobe was on an inside wall. Isabel ran to it, jerked the doors open, dropped to her knees, and frantically shoved the shoes out of her way.

"Hush now, hush now," she whispered as she reached up and ripped her thick robe off the hanger and pulled it down to cover the hard wood. She placed Parker on top, jumped back up, and pushed the doors together, leaving only a crack so that air could get inside.

Less than a minute had passed since the first gunshot was fired, but her mind was screaming at her to hurry, hurry, hurry. She ran back into the living room, doused the lights, and cocked her rifle. With her back against the wall, she slowly began to edge toward the curtains so she could look outside.

The front window suddenly exploded into a thousand fragments. Glass shattered across the room as more and more bullets pierced the walls and the floor. A candlestick bounced across the mantel, crashed to the rug, and rolled into the fireplace.

And then there was silence, and that was far more terrifying to her than the noise had been. Were they finished with their game, or were they reloading their weapons? If they were drunk, they'd get bored quickly and leave.

Please, God. Please, God. Make them leave.

She edged closer to the gaping hole that once was her window. With the tip of the rifle barrel, she lifted the shredded drape and looked out into the night.

It was as dark as death outside. Thunder rumbled in the distance as rain pelted her face and her neck. She strained to hear every little sound and waited for one of them to come toward her.

Suddenly the sky was lit up by a bolt of lightning and she saw all six of them clearly. They had formed a line in front of her door and were less than twenty feet away from her son.

Spear's face loomed out at her, and in the gray, crackling light, his skin had taken on a ghoulish tinge, and his eyes, oh, God, his eyes, were as red as a demon's.

She threw herself back against the wall and took a deep breath so she wouldn't scream. She would kill him first.

A voice lashed out at her with the force of a bullwhip slicing through the stillness.

"Remember me, bitch? My name's Spear, and I'm in charge now. I'm through waiting on you. You hear me? I'm going to count to ten, and if you don't want me to hurt you, you'll get outside before I'm finished."

His voice was cold, deliberate, and filled with hate. He didn't sound drunk, and that made him all the more dangerous. Liquor wasn't ruling his actions; evil was.

"One . . . two . . . three . . ."

"Wait, Spear," one of the others shouted. "Is that a baby bawling?"

"Son of a bitch," someone yelled. "She went and had the baby."

Douglas slowly turned the corner of the barn and moved up behind Spear. He was in such a rage now, he had to keep telling himself to take his time.

"One of us ought to go inside and take the baby. Then she'll follow us," the man on Spear's left suggested with a nervous giggle. "Go and get it, Spear. I ain't going in there and taking on that hellcat. You do it."

"I'll go get both of them," his friend said. "I'm not afraid." His boast was promptly followed by his scream. "I've been bit," he cried out. "I've been bit up my leg."

"What are you crying about, Benton? There aren't any snakes out tonight. You're just spooked, that's all."

Spear dismounted. "Both of you be quiet so I can hear the woman when she calls out."

"You think she's gonna invite you inside?" one of the men asked with a snicker.

Benton turned his mount and headed for the hills. Douglas could hear him sobbing as he rode away. He wondered how long it would take for the drunken fool to realize he had a knife lodged in the back of his thigh.

Spear was standing next to his mount, obviously trying to decide if he wanted to go inside or not.

Douglas hoped to God he'd try. Douglas wasn't going to let him get near that door, and if that meant killing him, Douglas wouldn't suffer any qualms. The bastard had terrorized an innocent mother, partially destroyed her home, and now believed he could drag her and her baby away with him. The mere thought of any of them touching Isabel or Parker sent Douglas into a black rage.

Move, Spear. Move.

Spear pulled his gun out of his holster, and that was a fatal mistake. He had taken one step toward the stoop when Douglas shot his right leg out from under him.

Damn, it felt good.

Spear didn't think so. He screamed as he went down to his knees. He frantically staggered back to his feet, whirled around, and swung his gun up to shoot.

Douglas shot the other leg out from under him. Spear fell forward, his gun clutched in his hand, and landed face first in the mud.

"Anyone else want to limp for the rest of his life?"

The venom in Douglas's voice, added to Spear's screams, was enough to convince the others to give up the fight.

Spear was wiggling around in the mud like a pig trying to keep cool. He shouted to his men to kill Douglas, as he rolled to his side, lifted his head, and took aim with his gun.

Douglas shot him in the center of his forehead. One of his friends went for his gun, but his hand never reached his holster. Douglas's next bullet cut deep into his shoulder. The man cried out and slumped forward.

"Throw your weapons on the ground," Douglas ordered.

He waited until they'd obeyed his command before he called out to Isabel. "It's over now. Are you and the baby all right?"

He could hear the fear in her voice when she answered him. "Yes, yes . . . we're fine."

A few seconds later, light from the kerosene lamp spilled out into the yard through the window.

"We've got friends waiting up in the hills, mister," one of the captives boasted. "If you've got any sense at all, you'll leave before they come riding down here and kill you."

"I'm guessing he's all alone," his friend whispered.

"Guess again, jackass."

The voice was Cole's. Douglas was so happy to hear it he began to laugh. He didn't have to turn around to know that his brothers were standing behind him. He hadn't heard them approaching and would have been disappointed if he had, for any sound would mean that they had gotten lazy. Being lazy in the West would get a man killed.

"What the hell took you so long to get here?"

"I had to round up the others before we could leave," Adam answered.

"Are you going to kill these men? You might as well since you've got your gun drawn and all."

"He isn't going to kill them, Cole."

"Glad you could make it, Harrison," Douglas said.

"You should let us go, mister. Benton already got away, and he'll tell the others."

"Lord, they're stupid," Adam said.

"I assume the man with the knife in his backside is Benton," Harrison said. "Travis went after him. He figured you'd want your good knife back."

Douglas tossed his shotgun to Cole. "Tie them up inside the barn."

The cabin door suddenly flew open and Isabel came running outside with her rifle in her hands.

Douglas moved forward into the light. He took the rifle away from her so that she wouldn't accidentally shoot one of his brothers. He knew she'd seen them because she'd come to an abrupt stop and was staring beyond his shoulder, but after giving each one of them a quick glance, she turned her attention to Boyle's henchmen.

"Where is he?" she asked, her voice shaking with anger.

"Who?" Douglas asked.

"Spear. Did you kill him? Never mind. I don't care if he's dead or not. I'm going to shoot him anyway."

Douglas wouldn't let her have her rifle back. He made sure the safety was on, then threw it to Adam. "You don't want to shoot anyone."

"Yes, I do. I want to shoot all of them."

She grabbed hold of his shirt and held tight. "I'm going to shoot someone, Douglas. They . . . woke . . . my . . . baby . . . and they . . ."

She couldn't go on. The horror of what she had just gone through suddenly struck her full force. She collapsed against him and began to sob.

"We'll leave here, Douglas. I won't fight you any longer. We'll leave . . . We'll leave."

Twelve

❧

The Simpson kitchen was crowded with Claybornes. Trudy Simpson was making a fresh pot of coffee for her honored guests. She was thrilled to have the men at her table and wanted to prepare a feast to show her appreciation. The brothers had come to Sweet Creek to help Isabel, and that made them exceptional.

The men spoke in whispers to one another so that Parker wouldn't be disturbed. He was sleeping peacefully up against Cole's shoulder.

The doctor joined them a few minutes later. He dropped a large packet of yellowed papers tied together with a pink ribbon on the table in front of Douglas.

"I took these away from Isabel. It's after one in the morning, and I found her poring over them when she should be sleeping. Why don't you go through them for her? One of the papers has to be the deed to that useless land, and when you find it, I think we ought to burn it, for all the good it's done."

"How is she feeling, Doctor?" Trudy asked.

"She's tuckered out, but otherwise just as fit as can be. You needn't be worrying about our girl."

"It's a miracle this little boy made it," she remarked. She put a platter of ham on the table and turned back to the counter to fetch the biscuits. "Why, he's no bigger than a minute. I don't believe I've ever seen a baby so tiny."

The doctor squeezed a chair in between Adam and Harrison and sat down. "He's not as small as I expected him to be, but he's got to stay put until he has more weight on him. Do you understand what I'm saying, Douglas? Isabel and her boy have got to stay here. Now, since you brought them to us, I'm wanting to know what you're planning to do when trouble comes calling."

"Meaning Boyle and his gunslingers?" Harrison asked.

Douglas had already told his brothers everything he knew about Boyle, and by the time he'd finished giving the details, they were all anxious to meet the man who had single-handedly terrorized an entire town. Cole was the most curious. He was also the most determined to end the tyrant's reign.

"I'll make certain the fight doesn't come into town," Douglas said.

"How are you going to do that?" Dr. Simpson wanted to know.

"Mrs. Simpson, will you please stop staring at me?" Cole asked. "You're making me nervous."

Trudy laughed. "I can't help it. You look just like I expected Marshal Ryan to look. You've got the same color of hair and eyes, and you're as big as he's supposed to be."

"But you've never seen Ryan, have you, ma'am?" he asked, his exasperation apparent.

"It doesn't make any difference. The minister gave us a fine description of the lawman, and almost every Sunday during his preaching time he's told us another story of Ryan's courage."

"Shouldn't he be preaching parables or something from the Bible? Why would he talk about Ryan?" Adam asked.

"To give us hope," Trudy answered. Her eyes got misty with emotion. "Everyone needs to have hope. And when Cole came strutting into my kitchen, I just naturally assumed he was Ryan. That's why I grabbed hold of him and kissed him."

"Ma'am, I don't strut. I walk. And I don't much like being compared to Daniel Ryan," Cole said.

"Why not? The man's a legend, for heaven's sake. Why, the stories we've heard about him, the tales of glory—"

"Begging your pardon, ma'am, but I don't think it's a good idea to tell Cole any of those stories now. He doesn't like the marshal. Fact is, he doesn't like him at all," Adam said.

Trudy's hand flew to her throat. "Oh, no, that can't be. Everyone likes him."

Douglas wasn't paying any attention to the conversation. He stared at the bundle of papers Parker Grant had left his wife. He didn't want to go through them, because every time he thought about her late husband, he became angry. Parker had subjected Isabel to hardships no woman should have to endure.

He shoved the packet across the table to his brother Adam. "You go through them. Pull out the important documents."

Adam immediately pushed the packet in front of Harrison. "You're the attorney. You go through them."

"Why does this have to be done now?" Harrison asked.

"Isabel wants to find the registration for the Arabians. She's got a mind to do something with the papers, but she won't confide in me. She can be stubborn, and you know how women can get a bug up their—"

"Doctor, watch your language please," Trudy reminded him.

"I was only going to say women get a bug up their sleeve, Trudy."

She snorted with disbelief. Her husband quickly changed the subject to avert an argument. "What did you do with those Arabians?" he asked.

"Travis had something in mind. We left it up to him," Adam explained. "Those sure are fine horses," he added with a nod.

Harrison was hunched over the table, reading documents. Douglas was explaining the change the doctor would have to make in his routine until Boyle was taken care of.

"You're going to have to stay here until this is resolved," he said.

"And just what will happen if anyone gets sick in the meantime? I have to go where I'm needed," the doctor argued.

"Then two of my brothers are going to go with you. Cole, you stay in town with Adam and make certain no one gets near this house."

"That's going to mean killing some of Boyle's men," Cole said.

"Then that's what you'll do."

"Who is Patrick O'Donnell?" Harrison asked.

The question caught the doctor's full attention. "Why in heaven's name would you be asking me about crazy Paddy Irish? Did you know him?"

"No, sir, I didn't know him, but his will is here, and his name is on this deed. I was wondering—"

Simpson wouldn't let Harrison continue. "Well now, son, I've got to tell you the story, just like I told Douglas, about Paddy Irish having the last laugh."

Douglas motioned for Harrison to hand him the
will and the deed so he could read them while the
physician retold the bizarre story about the crazy old
Irishman.

The brothers were fascinated by the tale. Douglas
was fascinated by the documents he held in his hands.
He was rereading the description of the property
Parker Grant had inherited from Patrick O'Donnell
but still couldn't accept what he was seeing until he'd
read the deed a third time.

Simpson had just finished his story when Douglas
began to laugh. He tried to explain why he was so
amused, but every time he began to speak, he was
overcome with laughter again.

"Son, you're making me think you're as crazy as old
Paddy Irish. What's got you so tickled?"

Douglas handed him the papers. Moments later,
Dr. Simpson was also overcome with laughter.

"Good Lord above, there's justice in this sorry
world after all," he said as he wiped the tears away
from his eyes.

"What's gotten into you two?" Trudy asked.

Cole stood up and began to pace around the kitchen
with Parker. The baby had been awakened by all the
commotion. "Lower your voices," he snapped. "Parker doesn't like it."

Adam got up and took the baby away from his
brother. "You've had him long enough. It's my turn."

"Paddy wasn't crazy, Trudy. Fact is, he was a very
clever man."

"And so was Parker Grant," Douglas acknowledged.

He leaned back in his chair and shook his head.
"Paddy filed a claim on a piece of land years before
Boyle came along and settled here."

The doctor picked up the story then. "Boyle never
did give the law a second thought. He liked to take
what he wanted. He still does," he thought to add.

"Well now, I reckon he'd only been here a little while when he decided to build himself a grand house on the top hill just outside of town.

"Everyone thought it was kind of peculiar the way Paddy would go out there every single day, rain or shine, to watch the progress being made. It took more than a year to finish it, almost two. Yes, sir, it did. The house was three stories high and had every fancy gadget inside you could ever imagine. A chandelier hanging in the dining room came all the way from Paris, France. Oh, yes, it was a palace all right, and Boyle meant to show it off."

"Where did he get the money to build such a grand house?" Adam asked.

"He rented out most of the land to those foreign barons who have gotten into the cattle business because it's so profitable. The cattle were driven up from Texas to graze on sweet Montana grass. He's made a bloody fortune over the years collecting his rent money."

"Only it wasn't his rent money. It was Paddy's. Paddy owned the land Boyle built his home on," Douglas explained.

"He must have told Boyle the night of the party, because that's when the beatings began. I had to patch Paddy up so many times I lost count."

"Why didn't Boyle simply kill Paddy?" Cole asked.

"Paddy must have gone to an attorney and had a will drawn up. He was smart enough not to taunt Boyle without having some sort of legal protection, and knowing how that crazy Irishman liked to have his fun, I imagine he refused to tell Boyle who would inherit the land after he died. He certainly wouldn't have told him where the will could be found. Paddy was a shrewd one all right."

"Who did inherit?" Adam asked.

"I don't know who he was going to leave everything to when he first had the will drawn up, but you can see from this amendment that he had the will changed after he met Parker and Isabel. Probably because they showed him such kindness, he gave it all to them."

"Then Isabel owns Boyle's house and all the land?" Travis asked.

"Yes," the doctor answered.

"The money Boyle collected from renting the land to the barons belongs to her too," Harrison interjected.

Douglas nodded. "Either Paddy told Boyle right before he died who the land would go to, or Parker told Boyle after Paddy had died. Either way, it was a mistake. Whoever it was should have used the law to force the claim."

"Boyle wouldn't have listened to the law," Simpson said.

Harrison disagreed. "A good attorney would have gotten a judge to confiscate the accounts at the bank. Boyle would have had to go into court and win before he could get his hands on the money again. He would have lost, of course, and poor men can't hire gunmen to do their dirty work."

All of a sudden, the Clayborne brothers were up and moving. Douglas and Cole both pulled out their guns at the same time and headed for the back door. Adam disappeared into the hallway with Parker, while Harrison stood in front of Trudy Simpson with his gun out.

Everyone waited in silence. Trudy jumped when a low whistle sounded from just outside the window.

A second later, Travis came strolling inside, looking weary but happy. He slapped Douglas on his shoulder as he passed him, tipped his hat to Mrs. Simpson before removing it altogether, and then sat down at the table.

Introductions were made, and Trudy did her best to make the latest addition to her table feel welcome.

"Are you hungry, young man? I believe I'll fix you a bite to eat."

"I don't want you to go to any trouble, ma'am."

Trudy had already turned away to fetch her skillet. The doctor poured Travis a cup of coffee and then sat down again. "You're going to eat, son, so you might as well accept it. My Trudy's got her mind set and her frying pan out."

"Yes, sir. I'll eat."

"Did you get my knife back for me?" Douglas asked.

"Yes. I tied Benton to a post inside the barn so he could drive the others crazy with his crying. I've never seen a man weep like that. Honest to God, it was disgusting."

Cole laughed. "We heard you coming up to the door, Travis. You're getting sloppy."

"I wanted you to hear me."

Adam came back into the kitchen with the baby. "Parker's hungry," he remarked.

Douglas immediately got up, took the baby into his arms, and headed for the steps.

Trudy chased after him. "Now, hold on, Douglas. You can't go barging into Isabel's room. It wouldn't be proper."

"Trudy, he delivered that baby," her husband called out. "I don't believe it's going to matter if he sees her in her nightgown now. He's been living under her roof for over two months."

"That was then, and this is now," Trudy said. "Douglas, you had to deliver that baby because there wasn't anyone else around to do it. Things have to be more proper now though. I'll take the baby up."

She wiped her hands on her apron before taking the baby away from Douglas. He didn't give her any argument, for he knew that it would **probably be better for Isabel if she didn't see him again. He had** hurt her by making her face reality. In time, she would realize he had taken advantage of her, and he hoped to God that when that day came, she wouldn't hate him.

He leaned against the wall, folded his arms across his chest, and stared off into space as he tried to imagine what his life was going to be like without ever seeing Isabel or Parker again.

Harrison pulled him out of his bleak thoughts. "You delivered the baby?"

"Yes."

"Sit down and tell me what it was like."

"Why?" Adam asked.

"I want to be prepared for my son or daughter's birth. I'm a little . . . nervous about it. I don't like the idea of my wife having pain."

Douglas was thankful for the diversion. He straddled the chair to face Harrison. "You're nervous? I didn't think anything ever got to you."

Harrison shrugged. "Tell me what it was like," he demanded.

Douglas decided to be completely honest. He leaned forward and whispered, "Sheer hell."

"What did he say?" Cole asked.

"He said it was sheer hell," Adam repeated. "Stop joking, Douglas. Harrison's turning gray."

The brothers found that fact hilarious. Douglas thought he had pretty much summed up the experience, but upon reflection he realized it had only been hell for a little while.

"It wasn't bad," he said. "I was scared at first, and then I was too busy to think about everything that could go wrong. Isabel did all the work, and when I held Parker in my hands . . ."

The brothers were waiting for him to finish. Douglas shook his head. He didn't want to share the memory. It belonged to Isabel and him, and it was all he would be able to take away with him when he left Sweet Creek.

"It was pretty miraculous, Harrison," he admitted. "So stop worrying. Besides, you won't have to do anything. Mama Rose will help with the delivery."

"I plan on being with my wife when the time comes."

Trudy returned to the kitchen for the coffeepot, then circled the table refilling their cups.

"Thank you," Cole said. "You know what I don't understand?"

"What?" Adam asked.

"The folks in Sweet Creek," Cole said. "How can so many cower to one man?"

"One man with twenty-some gunslingers working for him," the doctor said. "There aren't any cowards in Sweet Creek, but most of the men are ranchers. None of them could hold their own in a fight because they don't have the expertise. Just ask poor Wendell Border."

"What happened to him?" Adam asked.

"Wendell was coming out of church with his wife and two little girls when some men grabbed him. They forced him to kneel down in front of Sam Boyle. Wendell wouldn't beg for mercy, and that was when Boyle ordered them to break both of his hands. Folks tried to stop what was happening, but the hired thugs had their guns out and threatened to kill anyone who got in their way. Poor Wendell's family had to watch. It was a sorry day all right."

"Now do you understand why I was so overcome with joy when I thought you were Marshal Ryan, Cole?" Trudy asked. "You seemed to be the answer to our prayers."

Travis's eyes widened. "I bet you just loved being mistaken for Ryan," he said.

"Everyone in town is going to make the same mistake I made," Trudy insisted.

It was this innocent remark that gave Douglas his

plan. Dr. Simpson was excusing himself when Douglas turned to him.

"Doctor, is there a jail in Sweet Creek?" Douglas asked.

"Yes. It's at the opposite end of town, near the stables. No one's been inside since the old sheriff put his badge on his desk and left town. Why do you want to know about the jail?"

"Cole's going to be using it," he replied. "I don't think you'll want to hear any more details, sir. It could get you into trouble with the law."

"All right then," the doctor agreed. "Come on, Trudy. The men need some privacy now. I've got a feeling tomorrow's going to be a hard day for all of us. We might as well get some sleep now while we can."

Douglas waited until the elderly couple had gone upstairs before he told his brothers what he wanted to do.

"Mrs. Simpson told me that everyone in town has been praying for Daniel Ryan to come and save them."

"And?" Cole asked.

Douglas grinned. "Tomorrow, their prayers are going to be answered."

Daniel Ryan, or rather Cole Clayborne masquerading as Daniel Ryan, came riding down the main street of Sweet Creek on Friday morning at precisely ten o'clock. He went directly to the telegraph office, where it was later reported he held a gun to Jasper Cooper's forehead to gain his cooperation in sending a wire to Samuel Boyle, informing him that his accounts had been confiscated.

At that very same moment, Harrison went inside the bank and presented to the officers in charge an impressive-looking document ordering them to remove all the money in Boyle's account to the bank of

Liddyville, where it would remain until the court determined ownership. The document was signed by a judge, but none of the officers could quite make out the signature.

The bank president, as it turned out, wasn't one of Boyle's followers. He didn't look too closely at the papers and didn't waste a minute transferring the money to Liddyville. He did do quite a bit of laughing though and, like Daniel Ryan, seemed to be having the time of his life.

Two of the cashiers helped print up a large sign, which they nailed to the hitching post outside the bank, notifying everyone that Boyle's money was gone.

Word spread like free whiskey, and within two hours at least fifteen of the twenty-five hired hands had left town for parts unknown. Their loyalty ran out with the money. Those who were determined to wait for Boyle to straighten out the situation were arrested by Marshal Ryan and two deputies, and duly locked in the jail.

None of what the Claybornes were doing was legal, a fact that Harrison pointed out at least a dozen times. Cole could get twenty years of hard labor for impersonating a lawman, and Harrison would be sharing the cell with him for falsifying documents.

Cole refused to worry about the consequences. It was his fervent hope that Ryan would hear he had an impersonator and come looking for him. Then Cole would finally get back the compass the lawman had taken from Mama Rose.

Douglas went after Boyle. He wouldn't let any of his brothers go with him and refused to give any details of what he planned to do. He asked Dr. Simpson to tell Wendell Border to bring his family to church the following Sunday, and to step outside at exactly eleven o'clock. There would be a surprise waiting for him.

Needless to say, that day the church was packed to the rafters. The Reverend Thomas Stevenson was thrilled to have a full house and decided to make the most of it. He threw out the sermon he'd prepared and preached about the fires of hell instead. He ranted, he raved, and he threatened. Anyone who failed to attend his church on a regular basis was doomed to spend eternity burning in hell. Oh, the reverend worked himself into a fine lather all right, screaming and pounding his fists on his pulpit while he worked the congregation into a frenzy of guilt and put the fear of God into their hearts.

He was right in the middle of screaming the word "damnation" when Wendell Border and his family stood up.

The preacher stopped in mid-shout. "Is it time then, Wendell?"

"It's going on eleven," Wendell called back.

The crowd waited in breathless silence for Wendell to leave his pew and lead the way outside. His wife held on to her husband's arm and walked beside him, while their two little girls skipped along behind.

In their wildest speculations, none of the townspeople could have guessed what was going to happen.

Coming down the center of the street toward the church was Sam Boyle. Douglas walked behind him and prodded him forward with the barrel of his shotgun.

Folks started laughing. Boyle didn't look so fierce now. He was dressed in dirty long underwear and nothing else. He hopped from bare foot to bare foot with his head down, and even though the laughter drowned out all other sounds, everyone could see that Boyle was crying.

No, he didn't look like much of a threat to anyone now, not even to the children. The bully had been revealed at last, and only the coward remained.

Dr. Simpson told Isabel later that Douglas had

found something better than death to punish Boyle with. He'd used his pride to destroy him.

Boyle cried all the way to the steps, then knelt down in front of Wendell and begged his forgiveness. Wendell wasn't in the mood to give it, and so he remained stubbornly silent.

The law-abiding citizens of Sweet Creek chased Boyle out of town. No one expected him to ever return, but if he did, they would measure out justice once again. His mantle of power had made him seem invincible to those he terrorized, but now the town had seen him for what he really was and stopped being afraid.

Peter Collins, the stableman, stepped forward to offer his services as sheriff. Cole, still masquerading as Daniel Ryan, took the time and trouble to swear him in.

The Claybornes left town a few hours later. Douglas left his heart behind.

Thirteen

❧

Getting on with life wasn't easy. Douglas kept busy every waking hour so that he wouldn't have time to think about Isabel. Business was booming, and folks from as far away as New York City came to Blue Belle to look over the magnificent horses the Clayborne brothers raised.

Douglas broadened his operation by purchasing additional land adjacent to the main ranch. The wild horses Cole and Adam captured were taken to the green pastures and trained there before they were also put up for sale.

The stable in Blue Belle was also expanded, as was a second stable Douglas had purchased on the outskirts of Hammond.

He worked from sunup to sundown, but time, distance, and backbreaking labor didn't ease the ache he felt whenever thoughts of Isabel intruded.

He told himself over and over again that he had done the right thing. Why then did it hurt so much?

His brothers stayed out of his way as much as possible. Adam dubbed him "The Bear," which, it was unanimously agreed, fit Douglas's gruff personality these days. He snapped at everyone but his Mama Rose and his sister, rarely smiled, and stubbornly refused to tell anyone what was bothering him.

His brothers had already figured it out, for they had met Isabel Grant, and after spending five minutes in the same room with her and Douglas, it had become apparent to them that their brother had fallen in love with the beautiful woman. She was soft-spoken, sweet-natured, and obviously much more intelligent than Douglas was. She didn't make any attempt to hide how she felt about their brother, which made them like her all the more. Douglas, on the other hand, was determined to act like a mule's backside. If *they* knew he loved Isabel, they figured *he* had to know it too, and just when was he going to come to his senses and do something about it?

Cole predicted it would take three months for Douglas to act and wagered five dollars that he was right. Travis bet it would only take two months, met Cole's five-dollar wager, and upped the ante to ten dollars. Adam thought it was disgusting that his brothers were wagering on Douglas's misery. He also thought it would take his brother four months to go after Isabel and matched Travis's twenty-dollar bet.

Douglas didn't know about the wagers. Six weeks had passed since he'd left Sweet Creek, and not a single day had gone by that he hadn't thought about Isabel and Parker. He didn't know how long he'd last before he gave in and went back.

He was just leaving Hammond to go up to an auction in River's Bend when he received a telegram from Adam telling him to come home.

Douglas assumed his sister had gone into labor

early. Mary Rose had made all of her brothers promise to be there for the delivery of her firstborn. She didn't need them to comfort her but was, in fact, far more concerned about her husband. It was up to her brothers to keep Harrison calm.

He arrived at Rosehill around three in the afternoon. The sun was beating down on his shoulders; he hadn't shaved in two days, and all he could think about was getting a cold drink and a hot bath.

He spotted Pegasus as he was riding down the last hill. The Arabian stallion was prancing about inside the corral. Douglas squinted into the sunlight and saw Adam and Cole sitting in the shade of the porch with their feet propped up on the railing.

He slowed his sorrel to a walk as he passed the corral. The barn door opened as he was dismounting, and Travis led Minerva outside.

"Isn't she a fine-looking horse?" Travis called out.

Douglas was numb with disbelief. His voice was hoarse when he called out, "How did they get here?"

Travis shrugged. "You'll have to ask Adam," he suggested. "He probably knows."

Douglas headed for the house. Before he could ask any questions, Adam offered him a cold beer.

"You look parched," he remarked.

"I think he looks kind of sickly," Cole said.

"How did they get here?" Douglas demanded.

"How did who get here?" Adam asked.

"The Arabians," he muttered.

"They probably walked some," Cole said.

"Probably galloped some too," Adam told his brother.

They shared a smile before turning back to torment their brother a little longer.

Douglas was leaning against the post, staring into the hall through the screen door. The agony Adam saw in his eyes made him feel guilty.

"Maybe we ought to tell him, Cole."

"I think he ought to suffer a little longer. He's been hell to live with for the last month and a half. Besides, I lost the bet, or will, just as soon as he sees her."

"She's here, then?"

"She was," Adam said.

"Where is she now?"

"You don't need to yell at us. We can hear you just fine," Adam said.

"Isabel Grant is a contrary woman," Cole remarked. "She looks so sweet and innocent, but she's got a dark side to her, Douglas, which is why I'm so partial to her. You need to understand what you're getting into before you go looking for her."

"What are you talking about. Isabel doesn't have a dark side. She's perfect, damn it. She's good and kind and . . ."

"Generous?" Adam asked.

"Yes, generous."

"I agree with you," Adam said. "But I also agree with Cole. The woman does have a dark side all right. She wants you to have the two Arabians because you were so helpful to her, and that makes her a downright generous woman. Don't you think so, Cole?"

"Sure I do," his brother said. "But she also came here to kill him," he reminded his brother. "She seems real determined too. Maybe I shouldn't have loaded the shotgun for her, Adam."

"Nope. I don't suppose you should have."

"Is she still here?"

Douglas was moving toward the door when Adam answered. "Yes, she's here."

"If she kills you, we still get the Arabians," Cole called out. "Isabel promised us."

Douglas had already gone inside. He searched the upstairs, looked in the parlor, the library, the dining room, and then went into the kitchen. Mama Rose was standing at the stove. She turned as he entered the room, and that was when he saw Parker in the crook of her arm.

He came to a dead stop and simply stared at the baby.

"Isn't he about the sweetest little thing you've ever seen, Douglas? Why, he smiles all the time. Just look at him. He's smiling now."

Douglas reached out to touch the baby. The tips of his fingers brushed over the top of his head.

Parker looked up at him and smiled.

"Where's his mother?" he asked, his voice rough with emotion.

"She was headed for the barn," Mama Rose said. "I'd be careful if I were you. She's upset with you."

Douglas was suddenly smiling. "So I heard."

He went out the back door, turned the corner of the house, and ran toward the barn. Cole called him back with a shrill whistle.

He turned around, and there was Isabel. She was standing on the top step watching him.

He suddenly forgot how to walk. He couldn't believe she was here. She looked as mad as a hornet and was, without a doubt, the most beautiful woman he had ever seen . . . or loved.

Honor be damned. Right or wrong, he was never going to let her go. He took a step toward her. She lifted the hem of her skirt and started down the stairs, but Cole stopped her.

"Don't forget your shotgun, Isabel."

"Oh, yes, thank you, Cole, for reminding me."

She picked up the weapon, turned around, and continued on. She stopped when she was about fifteen feet away from Douglas and put her hand up.

"Stop where you are, Douglas Clayborne. I have something to say to you, and you're going to listen."

"I've missed you, Isabel."

She shook her head. "I don't think you missed me

at all. I waited and waited, but you didn't come for me, and I was so sure that you would. You hurt me, Douglas. I needed to come here and tell you how cruel you were to leave me. Everything you said to me before you left . . . Do you remember? I remember every word. You told me I had to rejoin the outside world and that I would eventually forget all about you. Well, you were wrong about that. I'll never forget you. Will you forget me?"

"No, I could never forget you. Isabel, I was going to—"

She wouldn't let him finish. "You never told me you loved me, but I know that you do. I told you how I felt. Remember? I loved you then, I love you now, and I will go on loving you until the day I die. There, I needed to say that too. I hope you're as miserable as I am, you stubborn, pigheaded mule."

He took a step toward her. She backed up and put her hand up again. "Stand still, and let me have my say. I've only just gotten started. I've saved all this up for a long time, and you're going to listen. How dare you tell me I took you into my arms and my heart because I felt obligated to you. I was furious that you would believe such a thing, but then, the longer I thought about it, the more I realized how right you were."

He was taken aback by her admission. "No, I wasn't right," he said.

"Yes, you were," she replied. "I did feel obligated to you, and that was surely why I slept with you. Love didn't have anything to do with it."

"Isabel, you can't really believe—"

"Will you stop interrupting me? I need to finish this. After you left, I had plenty of time to think things over, and I realized I also felt obligated to dear Dr. Simpson. Yes, I did, and so I slept with him. Trudy didn't mind. Then I realized I also felt obligated to Wendell Border. The man tried to get help for me, after all. This isn't funny, Douglas, so you can stop smiling."

"Did you sleep with Wendell?"

"Yes, I did," she said. "His wife was very understanding. The Arabians belong to you. They can't be separated, and Parker did sell Pegasus to you. Besides, I don't have any place to keep them."

"You own half of Montana," he reminded her.

"No, the orphanage owns half of Montana. The sisters should be moving into Paddy's grand house any day now with the children. They'll be self-sufficient and have a nice income from the rents they collect on their grazing land. I made the sisters promise to call their new home Paddy's Place. They wanted St. Patrick's Place, but I got my way."

"You gave it all away? What about your son? How are you—"

"My baby and I will be just fine. I'm going to teach at the school and will make enough money to support the two of us."

"Isabel, I really need to kiss you."

"No," she said. "I haven't finished with my obligations. I realized I was beholden to your brothers. They were very helpful, if you'll recall, and I am going to sleep with each one of them too. It's only fair. When I'm finished, I'm going to come out here and shoot you for being so stubborn." She put the shotgun down and tried to walk away. "Cole? May I have a few minutes of your time?" she called out.

Douglas was laughing when he grabbed her hand and pulled her toward him.

"I love you, Isabel. I loved you then, I love you now, and I'll love you until the day I die. We're like your Arabians, sweetheart. We can't be separated. I've been so damned miserable without you and Parker. I don't want to get over loving you, and the only man you're ever going to be obligated to is me. Ah, sugar, don't cry. I was coming to get you. I couldn't fight it any longer. Being away from you and Parker was making me crazy."

"I'm leaving you this time."

He wrapped his arms around her, leaned down, and kissed her. "No, you're not leaving. We belong together, now and forever."

She put her arms around him and let him kiss her again. "Are you through being stupid, then?"

He laughed again. "Yes," he promised.

"I'm still going back to Sweet Creek, and you'd better follow me. God help you if you don't. You're going to court me and take me to tea parties and dances. I don't care if you want to or not."

"I've got a much better idea. Marry me, sugar."

Pocket Books celebrates
Julie Garwood's new Clayborne series
with a $2.00 rebate

JULIE GARWOOD

OFFICIAL MAIL-IN OFFER FORM

To receive your $2.00 REBATE CHECK by mail,
just follow these simple rules:

- Purchase all four books in the Clayborne series by March 31, 1998.
Titles include: **ONE PINK ROSE** (June paperback), **ONE WHITE ROSE**
(July paperback), **ONE RED ROSE** (August paperback)
and **COME THE SPRING** (December hardcover).

- Mail this official form (no photocopies accepted) and the proof of
purchases (the back page from each paperback book that says "proof of
purchase" and the clipped corner from the inside front jacket flap of the
hardcover that shows the product price and title) from each of the following
books: **ONE PINK ROSE, ONE WHITE ROSE, ONE RED ROSE** and
COME THE SPRING (hardcover). Also include the original store cash
register receipts for each book, dated on or before March 31, 1998, with
the purchase price of each Julie Garwood Clayborne series title circled.

All requests must be received by April 8, 1998. This offer is valid in the United States
and Canada only. Limit one (1) rebate request per address or household. You must
purchase a paperback copy of each of the following Julie Garwood titles: **ONE PINK
ROSE, ONE WHITE ROSE,** and **ONE RED ROSE** and the hardcover copy of **COME
THE SPRING** in order to qualify for a rebate, and cash register receipts must show
the purchase price and date of each purchase. Requests for rebates from groups,
clubs or organizations will not be honored. Void where prohibited, taxed, or
restricted. Allow 8 weeks for delivery of rebate check. Not responsible for lost, late,
postage due or misdirected responses. Requests not complying with all offer
requirements will not be honored. Any fraudulent submission will be prosecuted to
the fullest extent permitted by law.

Print your full address clearly for proper delivery of your rebate:

Name_____

Address_____Apt #_____

City_____ State_____ Zip_____

Mail this completed form to:

Julie Garwood's Clayborne Series	In Canada mail to:
$2.00 Rebate	Julie Garwood's Clayborne Series
P.O. Box 9266 (Dept. 7)	$2.00 (Can.) Rebate
Bridgeport, NJ 08014-9266	Distican 35 Fulton Way
	Richmond Hill, Ont L4B 2N4

1324
(2 of 2)

Proof-of-Purchase

One
White
Rose

1325